Joan Silver
and
Linda Gottlieb

limbo

PUBLISHED BY POCKET BOOKS NEW YORK

LIMBO

Viking Press edition published February, 1972

POCKET BOOK edition published June, 1972

This POCKET BOOK edition includes every word
contained in the original, higher-priced edition. It is printed
from brand-new plates made from completely reset, clear, easy-to-read
type. POCKET BOOK editions are published by POCKET BOOKS, a division
of Simon & Schuster, Inc., 630 Fifth Avenue, New York, N.Y. 10020.
Trademarks registered in the United States and other countries.

L

"There is absolutely no reason to believe Roy is dead. Roy is missing.... Until there is a cessation of hostilities over there—even if it takes ten more years—or until we have specific proof to the contrary, we will carry your husband as Missing in Action. ...Feel better?"

With these words, Colonel Lloyd, head of Chester Air Force Base's Casualty Office, hastens to assure twenty-one-year-old Sandy Lawton that the limbo in which she has been living for the last two years will certainly continue. Sandy and the other women who belong to "the club nobody wants to join" are wives of prisoners of war or men missing in action in Indochina. **LIMBO** is the moving story of their personal experiences, set against a backdrop of a burgeoning antiwar movement and the pervasive sexual revolution.

Out of the silent crisis of hundreds of women in real life whose husbands are missing in Vietnam, Joan Silver and Linda Gottlieb have written a poignant, urgent novel of women confronted by pressures unknown to the wives of POWs in any other war.

Serialized in *McCall's* Magazine, a Literary Guild alternate, **LIMBO** will soon be released as a major motion picture by Universal Pictures and will be directed by Mark Robeson, who directed *Peyton Place*.

LIMBO
was originally published by The Viking Press, Inc.

For Ray and Paul

limbo

"Bluejay Lead. I'm hit! I'm hit!"

"Roger, Bluejay Two. How bad are you?"

"I gotta leave it."

"Roger. We'll cover for you. . . . Can you make it to the ridge?"

"Don't know. I'll try. . . ."

The telex came in from Saigon. Casualty immediately swung into operation. "Find out who's next of kin," the major ordered. "His wife, sir," the lieutenant replied. "Let's go, then," he said. "Call the chaplain." The major stuffed the telegram into his brief case. "Get her address, she'll be at work now." He headed toward the door. It was 0955.

He pulled up both armrests, leaned his head back against the seat and put his feet into the stirrups. "Lead, I'm gonna blow the canopy," he radioed.

"Roger, Bluejay Two. See ya around."

He pressed a button and the glass cover flew off above his head. He pushed the trigger on his armrests. The seat shot up into the air, his body still attached to it. The wounded bird sped away under him and he began falling now. Beep, beep, beep. The emergency signal was activated.

"Let's get started." The major stood in the parking lot, looking at his watch. The medic hurried to the car and settled himself in the driver's seat. The major and the chaplain got in opposite sides of the back seat, and the

1

Air Force blue sedan streaked toward the gates of Chester Air Force Base.

Beep, beep, beep. . . . He pulled the ripcord and felt the chute check his fall. The ridge was still up ahead of him. Floating. He felt himself floating downward. Beneath him was a thick, impenetrable blanket of trees. The jungle of North Vietnam. Beep, beep, beep. . . .

"You got the directions?" the major asked the medic. "Yes, sir." They passed the Ocean Breeze Miniature Golf Course, Swank Cleaners, Reliable Roofers (We're on Top of Everything), Dairy Delite. There was little conversation in the car. The major thought to himself, I'll never get used to it. No matter how many times, I'll never get used to it.

The A-1s were in looking for him. Nearby the Jollys were hovering in a safe orbit, waiting until the A-1s found him before going in. "Bluejay Two, this is A-1 Lead, do you hear me?"

Beep, beep. . . . The beeper stopped.

"Bluejay Two, this is A-1 Lead. If you hear me, use your beeper or come up guard." The A-1 pilot searched methodically, flying in ever-increasing squares over the silent, unruffled green canopy.

"We turn off here," the medic said. He clicked on his right-hand signal, checked his mirror, and made a smart turn off the highway. It was a beautiful, clear day. The time was 1052.

"This is A-1 Lead, to all craft. This is A-1 Lead, to all craft. Return to base. Repeat. Return to base. Bluejay Two unlocatable."

1

On the morning of October 14, 1967, Sandy Lawton
placed a blue-and-white checked scarf loosely over her
blond beehive hairdo, tied the ends under her chin,
lowered the top of her white convertible and started out
on the daily trip from Chester Air Force Base to the
Community National Bank. She beeped dum-da-dum-dum
to Smitty, on guard duty at the gate, who snapped an
exaggerated salute back to her. Grinning, she flicked the
car radio to her favorite rock station and pulled onto the
highway.

*Slow down, you move too fast. . . . Ya gotta make the
morning last* . . . Simon and Garfunkel crooned into the
sun-filled Florida air. Sandy hooked her thumbs around
the inside of the steering wheel and slapped her fingers
against the outside of the red rim in syncopated rhythm.
The click of her wide gold wedding band punctuated the
song. *Lookin' for fun and feelin' groovy.* . . . With her

3

right hand she reached down and opened her white straw pocketbook topped with maroon plastic cherries, took out a pack of Juicy Fruit, peeled off two sticks, saving the wrappers, and popped them in her mouth.

The car passed by Motel Row, as she called the strip of green-and-white bungalows and faded pink stucco sleeping palaces, each dressed up by a palm tree in front. Two glowing white-haired people beamed down at her from a billboard. "Golden age is fun at Leisure Village," they promised. Simon and Garfunkel were winding up. *Feelin' groovy . . . groovy . . . groovy.** Her white-sandaled foot gave the accelerator an extra push with each "groovy." She felt good. Yesterday she had received a long tape from Roy.

Pulling into the bank parking lot, she stopped the car. While the top was going up, she took the gum out of her mouth, placed it in the wrappers she had saved, and wedged the neat little yellow paper ball in the car ash tray next to five similar little yellow balls. Then she undid her scarf, folded it into her pocketbook and pinned on her oversized Community National yellow plastic daisy. "Hi There!" it said. "I'm Sandy Lawton. Glad to See You."

Since it was a Friday, she had a heavy number of pay-roll checks, as well as the usual assortment of money orders, Christmas club payments, and penny collections. In between transactions she glanced down at the counter at the picture of Roy, his dark eyes looking out at her so gravely from under his Air Force cap. Two more months until she joined him on his R and R in Hawaii.

She took her coffee break with Alice Jacuski, a mousy redhead from Accounts Receivable, who had found in Sandy a perfect friend at work. Not only was Sandy all-American cute, thereby lending a certain fallout to Alice; Sandy was also uninterested in dating, so that Alice's lack of conversational input on this subject was in no way a barrier to their friendship.

* "The 59th Street Bridge Song (Feelin' Groovy)." © Paul Simon 1966. Used with permission of Publisher.

"Want to go to Wayland's tonight, San?" Alice asked. "They're having a sale on bell-bottoms."

"Sure, terrific." Sandy shoved a piece of apple Danish in her mouth and sipped some hot coffee. Now that Roy was gone, she almost never made breakfast. No point in dirtying dishes just for one.

"Okay, meet you at five and we'll go. And, Sandy," she added, "maybe afterward we'll stop for pizza?"

"Sounds good to me," Sandy agreed.

"Yeah," Alice giggled. "Let's go all the way."

At exactly five after eleven, Mr. MacAfee, the manager, came up to Sandy's counter. He waited until she had finished counting out Mrs. Firth's social security money and then put his hand on her arm. "Sandy, would you mind coming with me for a minute? I think you'd better close your window."

"Sure thing, Mr. MacAfee." Community National had just instituted a Be Friendly campaign, and cheerfulness was a high-priority item. She shoved the "Please Use Next Window" sign in place, slid off her high stool and followed Mr. MacAfee down the green-carpeted halls to his office. At the door he stepped aside. "There are some people to see you," he said, looking away from her. She noticed that he was speaking faster than usual and seemed embarrassed. He held the door open for her and shut it behind her.

Standing erect, like overgrown book ends on either side of Mr. MacAfee's desk, were two Air Force officers. Sandy felt an electric shock flash down the length of her body.

The taller of the two officers reached out his hand. "Mrs. Lawton, I'm Ralph Rydell, and this is Chaplain Newcomer. We're with the Casualty Division over at Chester. Would you like to sit down?"

She felt the blood pounding somewhere behind her eyes. "Is he dead?" she blurted.

"Your husband's present determination is missing in action somewhere over North Vietnam," Major Rydell replied.

Sandy felt her knees buckle. The chaplain quickly pulled up Mr. MacAfee's brown leather visitor's chair beneath her. "Are you feeling faint?" he asked. "We have a medic in the car." Sandy shook her head.

Major Rydell snapped open his black leather brief case, pulled out a two-page telegram and began reading. "It is with great regret that we inform you that Lieutenant Roy Lawton . . ."

Sandy didn't hear the rest. She concentrated on a fly hopping around the glass cover on Mr. MacAfee's desk. She wondered how it had gotten in since the windows were sealed for air conditioning.

That weekend she stayed close to her apartment, and the following Monday, Tuesday, and Wednesday she did not go in to the bank. Sandy wanted to be sure they would have no trouble reaching her when the telegram arrived saying that Roy was found.

Major Rydell had driven her back to the base that Friday. She had sat silently next to him on the front seat of the car she and Roy had jokingly christened "Roy's Baby." It was a white Corvair with red bucket-seats, the extravagant wedding present to each other that they were still paying off. Roy used to pilot it down the highways, pretending it was his F–4 on a mission, smoothly careening around enemy cars and laughing at Sandy as she squealed in terror. "Don't worry, honey," he'd say, "I could drive this baby with my eyes closed," and she believed him.

Major Rydell pulled the car into Sandy's slot in front of the row of pale-green stucco apartments reserved for junior officers' families. "You'll be assigned a casualty officer soon, Mrs. Lawton," he had told her, "probably Tony Vinza. He's a good man, and he'll help you over as many of the rough spots as possible. And, of course, if there's anything we can do to help you, just holler." He opened the door on his side of the car. "After all, that's what we're here for."

"Thanks," Sandy nodded. Major Rydell handed her the keys, walked back to the blue Air Force sedan in which Chaplain Newcomer and the medic had driven over, and with a slight wave to her, pulled away.

She let herself into her apartment and sat down in the corner club chair, fingering the bumpy brown fabric shot with shiny gold threads. "This is my chair," Roy had said, settling himself in it the night before he left. "It's the daddy chair," he announced in mock seriousness, placing his arms on its overstuffed arms and puffing out his chest. Sandy had laughed and lunged for his lap. He had crumpled up and hugged her. "I guess I'll let ya use it while I'm gone." He held her very tight and neither of them had spoken.

It was impossible that he was lost, she told herself. Roy always knew where he was going and how to get there. If anyone could re-establish contact and get picked up, he could. She was sure of it. The Air Force even planned for such eventualities, she knew. Debby Jansen's husband jumped from helicopters to rescue downed pilots. That was his job; he was paid to do nothing else. Maybe when they found Roy, they would let him come home early. She got up and began to straighten the living room.

By evening, the full social machinery of the base had swung into operation. Rose McClung and Debby Jansen brought her a covered-dish supper of creamed chicken and peas. "It'll keep for days and you won't have to cook," Rose had said. "All you have to do is fix a little rice."

"They'll find him, San," Debby had reassured her. "Hell, maybe it's even a mistake. You hear about those things all the time. Afterward they tell you they're sorry."

The Chester wives were like Air Force wives anywhere —ardent bridge players and frequently more ardent drinkers, loyal companions to each other during the long stretches their husbands were away, feeding endlessly on the base's closed circuit of gossip. In a crisis, to live among them was to be ringed by an emotional fortress.

"C'mon, kiddo," Debby had said to her on Tuesday. "It's our bowling night. There's no reason for you just to sit around here." It had been five days and she had heard nothing. A week, she told herself, fighting down the beginnings of panic, it would not be unusual for it to take a week to pick him up. She grabbed a sweater and went along with Rose and Debby.

"If I score above 110, it means they'll find him," she told herself, shifting her fingers around in the heavy black ball to get a better grip and carefully sighting the pins. She was in top form that frame, breaking her previous record of 120. "Great, Sandy!" Rose had thumped her on the back.

Later, they had all gone over to the Officers' Club, sat around the black formica tables, played the juke box, and had their usual vodka stingers. It seemed like any other Tuesday.

"You girls are the best friends a person could have," Sandy told them as she sipped her drink and listened to Frank Sinatra singing "Strangers in the Night." "I don't know what I'd do without you."

When she let herself back into her apartment at the end of the evening, she felt buoyed by Debby and Rose's reassurances and soothed by the warm, protective night air of Chester.

On Wednesday, a telegram did come. Sandy opened it eagerly.

REGRET TO INFORM YOU WE ARE CALLING OFF AIRBORNE SEARCH FOR LIEUTENANT ROY D LAWTON DOWNED 14 OCTOBER 1967 HAVE COMBED AREA FOR FIVE DAYS WITHOUT SPOTTING TRACE OF HIM ENEMY FIRE AT OUR AIRCRAFT NOW VERY INTENSE MUST CONCLUDE HE IS MISSING IN ACTION POSSIBLY PICKED UP BY ENEMY OF COURSE WILL CONTINUE TO PRESS ALL EFFORTS TO DETERMINE HIS WHEREABOUTS

For the first time since last Friday it occurred to Sandy Lawton that she might never see her husband again. She sat down in Roy's chair, the telegram in her hand, and felt her fragile defenses of the past five days crumble apart.

A month later, Colonel Robert Lloyd, head of the Chester Casualty Division, asked Sandy to stop by his office on her way to work. She seated herself on the green simulated leather couch, carefully pulling down her red plaid skirt to almost touch her knees, anchored it in place with her bag, and waited for Colonel Lloyd, who was pouring coffee from the carafe on his hot plate into two large mugs. "I drink the stuff all day long," he said, offering her one. "I figure it'll be just my luck to go through combat in two wars and end up dead of caffeine poisoning."

She smiled. He was nice, with his white hair framing a golf-tanned face, his tortoise-shell glasses held together at one temple with adhesive tape. Colonel Lloyd might be head of the Casualty Office, but somehow he didn't seem "official." He looked competent yet warm. She had a vision of hundreds of men like this tracking down Roy, using radar, clerical papers, or machetes, whatever was necessary in a relentless, efficient search for her husband.

"Tell me, Sandy— May I call you Sandy?"

"Sure."

"Tell me how you're getting along." He stirred the sugar in his coffee and sat down next to her on the couch.

"I'm all right," she said, partly because it was an easy thing to say and partly because she wasn't sure how she felt.

"Yes, well, it takes a while to get your bearings, doesn't it? Most of our families tell me the first month is the hardest." He took a sip of coffee. "Not that it gets any easier, but you get a little more used to it, I guess. I'm sorry, did you want any sugar or cream?"

"Oh, no. Thanks." She shook her head.

"Sandy," he continued, "I called you in here because I wanted to assure you personally that even though the air search was called off, the Air Force will not relent in its efforts to locate Lieutenant Lawton."

"Great." Sandy nodded her head enthusiastically.

"I want you to know also that the Administration is taking steps—diplomatic measures and other steps which I'm not even privileged to discuss with you—in an effort to get your husband home. There is one way you can help those efforts."

"Yes?" Sandy sat forward on the couch.

"We strongly suggest that you say nothing to anyone about his being missing in action. If anyone other than the immediate family asks, we feel it is best to say just that he is in Southeast Asia. You might add, if you feel more comfortable, that you haven't heard from him for a while. Going public with this could jeopardize our efforts, Sandy, and that would not be good for either you or Roy. This comes from the highest quarters. You with me?"

She nodded. "Sure, Colonel Lloyd. Of course."

"Good." He moved on to the next item. "Now I guess Tony Vinza told you that as far as we're concerned, your husband is still active duty military, and you'll receive the same paycheck as you have been all along. That includes combat and flight pay. Financially, you don't have a thing to worry about." He smiled and added, "You know, the Air Force takes care of its own."

She nodded. Sergeant Vinza, the short, puffy twenty-two-year-old casualty officer assigned to her case, had informed her of all this.

"At the same time," Colonel Lloyd continued smoothly, "your husband's slot in the squadron has to be filled. I know it sounds hard, but it's just one of those things."

"Right." She hadn't thought about it, but she supposed it made sense.

Colonel Lloyd took off his glasses, being careful not to dislodge their broken temple, and began to polish them with a handkerchief he took out of his pocket. "Of course, your quarters allowance will be reinstated and you can apply it to your house or apartment rental."

Maybe Sandy had not heard him correctly. "Colonel Lloyd, I don't have to move off the base, do I?"

"I'm afraid so," he said, looking down at his glasses which were now very clean. "We will have to ask you to relinquish your quarters for the new man and his family." He put his glasses back on and gave her a sympathetic smile. "We do have an arrangement with a very good real-estate broker, Mr. Talbot of Talbot and Jonas. He's tops at this sort of thing, and he'll have you fixed up in no time. Unless of course you prefer to live on another base. You *can* move onto any other base that has surplus housing, you know. Let's see." He moved over to his desk and opened up a manila folder. "At present we can offer you . . . Minot Air Force Base."

"Where is that?" Sandy asked.

"Minot, North Dakota."

"North Dakota! Colonel Lloyd, I don't want to go to North Dakota. I mean, Roy expects me to be *here*. And my job. I don't know anyone in North Dakota."

Colonel Lloyd nodded. "That's why I suggested putting you in touch with Mr. Talbot."

"How long do I have before I have to move off?" The perspiration was making her red sweater feel clammy under her armpits. She put the coffee mug down.

"Oh, say thirty days. I know how you feel, but we're so tight for space here. It's a damn shame," he said, standing up and escorting her to the door.

2

Letter from the Department of the Air Force

Dear Mrs. ——————,

Subject: Christmas Packages

. . . The contents of the packages should
be limited to recreational items, tobacco
items, small gifts made by children and the
like. . . . We do not recommend that you
include food items (with the exception of
instant coffee, tea, or powdered soft drinks
in nonbreakable containers) or vitamins as
this could conceivably jeopardize delivery of
the packages since North Vietnam has gone
to great lengths to proclaim to the world that
adequate food and medical treatment are
being provided to American prisoners of war.

Telegram to POW Wives from Department of the Air Force

IT IS A PLEASURE TO INFORM YOU THAT A
PACKAGE HAS BEEN FORWARDED TO YOUR
HUSBAND. THIS PACKAGE WAS PROVIDED BY THE
PILLSBURY COMPANY. A SIMILAR PACKAGE HAS
BEEN MAILED TO EACH PRISONER WHO HAS
CORRESPONDED WITH HIS FAMILY. ARRANGE-
MENTS FOR THE MAILING OF THESE PACKAGES

WERE MADE BY OUR STATE DEPARTMENT. WE
STRONGLY SOLICIT THAT YOU NOT REVEAL THE
CONTENTS OF THIS TELEGRAM TO ANYONE OUT-
SIDE YOUR IMMEDIATE FAMILY. PACKAGES
CONSIST OF DEHYDRATED FOODS AND VITAMINS
FOR APPROXIMATELY FIVE DAYS.

When Roy Lawton went down in the fall of 1967, there
were already 832 American men missing or captured in
Indochina, from every branch of the service. By the end of
1969 the number had swelled to 1451. Colonel Lloyd's
Casualty Division at Chester was now servicing the next
of kin of 21 of these men, all fliers. Some had gone down
over Laos, Cambodia, or Communist China, and these
men were simply never heard from. Others were taken
in skirmishes with the Vietcong in South Vietnam, and
if they were not killed immediately, were probably kept in
portable stockades, since the Vietcong were constantly on
the move. Occasionally the Vietcong acknowledged the
existence of some of these prisoners, though the names
they admitted to were probably only a handful compared
to the actual number they held. There was no way to get
more information, since the Vietcong were not the legal
government in the South, and thus there was no one to
talk to about such matters as captured prisoners. To be
taken by the enemy in South Vietnam, therefore, was not
desirable. By far the best place to fall into enemy hands,
ironically enough, was North Vietnam itself. If you made
it through the foliage and were not shot on sight or killed
by villagers who resented the bombs you had dropped,
you had a chance of sitting out the war in a prison camp
in what would be the longest captivity of prisoners in any
war in modern history.

One such fortunate flier was Brian Buell. In August of
1969 his wife, Mary Kaye Buell, was perched on a kitchen
stool in front of her breakfast counter reading and rereading a letter which had arrived earlier that day from the
Democratic Republic of North Vietnam. It was written in
pencil on a white onion-skin form edged with black and
was exactly seven lines long.

My dearest wife, I hope you are well, for I am. Hope
the boys are working hard in school, the girls
minding their mother and helping her. I pray
you are well and happy, I miss you darling, I
think about you and the children all the time.
It is cold here. Still no roommate. Someday
the good Lord will reunite us. Brian.

She lifted the receiver to call her mother-in-law in
Indiana. "Hello, Mother Buell. Yes, we're all fine, just
fine. Yes, the children are all fine. . . ."

In the living room Joe Buell, aged eleven, was blankly
whittling on a stick with a penknife, taking a certain
pleasure in seeing the shavings fall on the newly vacuumed
carpet. His ten-year-old brother, Pete, was aiming his
bow and arrow at a target propped up against a bridge
chair. "Bull's-eye!" he bellowed, as the suction-tipped
arrow thwacked to a halt.

"Hey, Pete, keep the noise down, I'm talking long
distance!" Mary Kaye took her hand off the mouthpiece
and continued talking to her mother-in-law. "Yes, we got
a letter from Brian this morning. . . . Of course, that's why
I'm calling. You want to hear it, dear?" With Brian's letter spread out in front of her and her eyes fixed on a
broken kitchen tile, which she had been meaning to fix,
Mary Kaye revised the contents of Brian's letter for his
mother. "Dear Mary Kaye, How is Mother? I think of her
constantly. I am in wonderful health and good spirits. The
food in this prison camp is really excellent."

"Don't cry, Mother Buell, don't you want to hear the
rest of it?" Mary Kaye glanced through the kitchen door
at the polychrome statue of the Virgin Mary rising out of
a grotto of artificial plants in the dining room as if to
say, "Don't judge me, I'm only trying to be good to his
mother."

"There's just another two lines, Mother. Listen: Kiss
the children for me and be sure to give Mother my dearest
love. Brian." Mary Kaye smiled slightly, content at the
pleasure she knew the tears had afforded her mother-in-
law. "No, Mother, you know I can't send you the letter.

The Air Force wants everything sent right on to Randolph as soon as it's received . . . All right, dear. Yes, I will. Bye-bye." She carefully folded the letter and put it in the pocket of her slacks, to be filed away later in the Pentaflex folder which compartmentalized all she had of Brian for the last four years.

At thirty-two, Mary Kaye had been married twelve years, less than half of them spent with her husband. For much of her married life, she had been alone while Brian was away on missions, or on extended tours in Vietnam and the Dominican Republic. For the last four years she had been the wife of a POW. Any way you looked at it, that was a lot of down time, she figured. Joe was born at Norton Air Force Base, Pete at Randolph, Kathy checked in the day the family arrived at McGuire, and Julie, now six and a half, was the Florida baby.

"Mommy, look, I found it!" Eight-year-old Kathy Buell emerged from the hall coat closet, one pigtail undone, triumphantly holding up a pencil holder made from an orange juice can. "It was way in the bottom of last year's Christmas presents for Daddy. Can we send it to him?" she begged her mother.

"A pencil holder! What does he need with a pencil holder, dummy?" Pete had wandered into the kitchen. "He probably only gets one pencil."

"You can use a pencil holder for just one pencil, can't you, Mommy?" The whine was beginning in Kathy's voice. "You said maybe we'd have room to put in one present."

"Yeah, but the whole thing can't weigh more than six pounds. We aren't going to use it up on that," Pete informed his sister.

"That's enough, mister," Mary Kaye snapped. "Here, Kath, give me the pencil holder." She took it from the little girl. "We'll see if we have room. I'm sure Daddy would love to have it, okay?"

" 'Kay." Kathy, mollified, settled down on the floor to a game of jacks with her sister.

Mary Kaye turned her attention to the large open carton on the kitchen counter which she was packing with items to send to her husband. She was pleased that she had been able to find instant coffee in paper packets. It cost a little more that way, but at least they wouldn't break in shipping. "Hey, Pete, stop clowning around with those— I need to pack them!" Pete reluctantly peeled himself out of the red thermal underwear Mary Kaye had selected for her husband. She lay the legs out on the counter, filled one with packets of Kool-Aid, the other with instant coffee, and the seat with a mixture of Tums, insect repellent, and sourballs. Carefully she folded it all up and placed the underwear on top of the other things.

Sourballs were not on the official Air Force list, but Brian always liked them, and there was something so impersonal about insect repellent. She could imagine him opening the package, putting on the warm underwear (he must be so thin now, she had bought a size smaller than he used to wear), tucking away the fungicide powder and Tums in a cubbyhole (she always imagined a cubbyhole next to his bed, the kind she had had in Girl Scout camp); and then taking a fistful of sourballs, the way he used to in the evenings, and popping two of them at a time in his mouth. Maybe he would think of her then, imagine her packing the carton as she was now. Maybe he would know that she was sorry.

"Hey, Ma, aren't we going to put in a picture this year?" Kathy asked.

"Good idea, Kath. Joe, go get the Polaroid, please," she called. Mary Kaye ushered everyone into the living room. "Joe!" She saw that he hadn't moved, and for the first time noticed the wood scrapings all over the floor. Hold on to your temper, she told herself, hold on. You've got to keep talking to him, it's the only way. "Kathy," she said, "run up and get the Polaroid. Joe," she kept her voice steady as he looked at her defiantly, "clean up the mess and come join us. We need you to take the first picture." Sullenly he picked up the shavings, one by one, as slowly as he could. "Then I'll take one with you in it too." Why, she wondered to herself, why did he behave this way?

"Julie, come sit on my lap on the couch. That way Daddy won't see how fat your old mother's gotten. Pete and Kathy, one of you on either side." Joe lethargically picked up the camera and aimed it at them. On the wall above, a square-jawed, pug-nosed man in Air Force uniform smiled out of his gilt frame and looked down on his family.

Mary Kaye stuck some wayward strands of dark hair into her pony tail and plastered the short pieces to her head with two bobby pins. She never wore lipstick or rouge. Her cheeks were naturally bright pink, and she always looked as if she had just come off the ski slopes or out of an argument. "An Irish complexion," Brian had called it. Her two brothers had the same coloring, pale white skin and highly colored cheeks. On a man it looked rugged and outdoorsy; to Mary Kaye, it lent the look of an overgrown child about to burst into a fit of temper, and indeed, when she did get angry, which was increasingly frequent these days, her cheeks would turn an even deeper red. She tucked her blouse into her slacks and shifted Julie slightly so that the child sat between the camera and the safety pin affixed to Mary Kaye's waistline.

"Cheese, everybody." The flash bulb went off, and Captain Brian Buell's Christmas photo for 1969 was officially recorded, in the living room of a house he had never seen.

Later that evening, after *I Dream of Jeannie,* including commercials and station identification, Mary Kaye went upstairs to tuck the girls into bed. She stood by their toy shelves, which consisted of old library shelving she had salvaged from the school where she taught sixth grade, and took down Snoopy.

"I want a story tonight, Mommy," Julie announced, snuggling up to the frayed stuffed dog and plugging her thumb in her mouth.

"No story tonight," Mary Kaye ruled, removing Julie's finger. "Joe's got too much homework, and I'm tired."

"Pete could read to us," Julie insisted.

"Dear heart, would that he could. Pete can barely read to himself. 'Night, Kathy." Climbing up the unpainted ladder to the upper bunk bed, Mary Kaye planted a kiss on her older daughter's cheek and smoothed out her long, copper-colored hair. As she climbed back down the ladder, she discovered that Julie was crying quietly in her bed.

"What's the matter, sweetheart? Julie, what is it? Don't you feel good?" she asked, bending down over the child.

Julie mumbled something into her pillow which Mary Kaye could not understand. "What is it, Julie, what's the matter?" She bent closer to the child.

"I . . . want . . . Daddy," the child sobbed. "I want to see my Daddy."

Mary Kaye felt the knots beginning in her stomach. She sat down on the bed. "I know you do, angel. We all want Daddy back home."

"But I want him *now*," Julie insisted, eyeing her mother accusingly.

Mary Kaye looked at her daughter with sympathy. Julie had been less than three when Brian went down. She must barely remember her father; yet more than any of the others, she cried for him.

"Julie dear, we'll all just have to wait a little longer to see Daddy," she explained patiently, but the sobbing continued. Mary Kaye sat on the bed for a few moments, helpless. Suddenly she felt herself becoming furious.

"Julie, that's enough," she yelled. "There's not a goddamn thing I can do to get your father back, so just shut up! Shut up!" She strode out of the room, slammed the door behind her and leaned against it, shaking. They get you, she thought. Kids really know how to get you.

When she went to bed that night, she dreamed they were making love in the king-sized bed she had bought specially for Brian's return. The only trouble was he insisted on keeping on his dog tags and Air Force hat. "Brian, wait Brian," she was saying to him, "not so fast. I have to tell you about Julie's tooth. Julie lost her first tooth." But he was kissing her and wouldn't listen. "Brian, you're their father. When your fourth child loses her first tooth, there's no one else who cares. Please listen." He moved over on top of her and reached his hand down for her to open her legs. "Hey, Bri, I thought you were in Hanoi." Still he said nothing, just purposefully moved between her legs. "I'm having trouble with Joe, Brian." She wished she could see his eyes, but the hat covered them. "Kathy had her First Communion, Brian. You would have been proud of her. She looked just like a bride." Her voice trailed off. She was beginning to respond now.

"Who's Kathy?" Brian inquired, removing his hat. To her intense surprise she found she was looking up at Phil Goratt, the gym teacher from school.

Mary Kaye sat up in bed, her body drenched with perspiration.

3

Letter from the Department of the Air Force

Dear Mrs. ——————————,

I am writing to inform you that photographic
analysis has determined that photograph
number 17 in the "Unidentified U. S. Prisoners of War in Southeast Asia" pamphlet
is of your husband. Because of the classifica-
tion of the pamphlet, we will be unable to
provide you a copy of the photograph. We
certainly appreciate your cooperation in this
matter.

The only noise in the room was the steady whirring of
the 16-millimeter projector. On the screen, blurred images
of three men in flight suits, hands held behind their heads,
jerked by. They were covered up almost immediately by a
patchwork of jagged dark shapes, and then the camera
swished free of the leaves and found the fliers again, this
time in profile and farther away. The men marched out of
the frame, and the grainy face of a North Vietnamese
guard came into view. He was holding a gun, hung from
his shoulder and aimed at the blurred men who had left
the picture. As he walked along the black-and-white for-
est, the film suddenly ran out. White circles, black leader,
and the voice of Colonel Lloyd. "Okay, Ryan, lights!"

The Chester Air Force Base film theater looked like any small-town RKO, except, as Mary Kaye Buell frequently pointed out to her casualty officer, it lacked a popcorn stand. A different feature was shown Mondays, Wednesdays, and Fridays, and Saturday was family day. This Saturday afternoon, however, the scheduled showing of *Mr. Magoo* had been canceled to allow all POW and MIA next of kin in the Tampa area to watch seven minutes of out-of-focus news clips taken in the jungles of North Vietnam.

"Sorry we didn't have any IDs on that one," Colonel Lloyd said, looking out at the mixed audience of wives, fiancées, mothers, fathers, sisters, brothers, and a few restless children. It was a good turnout, about fifty of them, he figured, which meant that Vinza and Slayback were doing their jobs. "I don't care if one of those gals is up in Walla Walla visiting her Aunt Tillie," he had told his two casualty officers. "You call her long distance. I want every next of kin notified personally. If they don't want to come, that's their business, but you better make goddamn sure they've been notified."

Colonel Lloyd stood now in the middle of the stage, clutching his mike in one hand and mopping his forehead with the other. The air conditioning had broken down and everybody at Maintenance seemed suddenly to be AWOL. "While we're waiting for the next film to be threaded up, I think I'll ask our casualty officers to serve some cold drinks before we have some real casualties on our hands." A polite chuckle from the audience. Colonel Lloyd smiled appreciatively and flashed a look at Sergeants Vinza and Slayback, who had already unglued themselves from the side of the stage and were hurrying out of the room. "Sorry about the air conditioning, folks. We've been trying to get it fixed all morning. It's hard to get the Air Force to move fast, but I can definitely promise you it'll be ready by our next film session." He beamed out at them. Bob Lloyd hadn't been selected for this position for nothing: as his superiors had noted all through his dossier of twenty years in the service, Lloyd was "good with people."

In the audience Carole Bogin leaned over to Sandy Lawton. "I wish they'd skip the small talk and just show the film." Sandy nodded. This October it would be two years since Roy went down. Over those years she had attended eight film identification sessions and strained her eyes at thousands of pictures in "The Book," as it was known, the bulging scrapbook containing all known photographs of prisoners held in North Vietnam, culled from world-wide sources and passed from base to base. Next of kin could then, in an orderly fashion, ink in their claims to the ears, backs, necks, and, occasionally, faces of the men pictured. In all that time Sandy had never seen a trace of Roy.

She had cut her hair so that it now framed her face closely, straight and unglamorous, easy to take care of. Otherwise she looked much the same as she had two years ago at nineteen, except that her gray eyes had lost their animated quality and at next-of-kin meetings Carole Bogin noticed that Sandy seemed not to hear things the first time. Sandy sat forward a little on her chair so that the itchy maroon plush of the seat would not touch her bare thighs. She felt nervous, dammit. Eight times she had been through this and still each time she felt nervous.

"All right, while our good sergeants are passing out refreshments, let me give you the fact sheet on the second film," Colonel Lloyd continued. He chug-a-lugged the Coke which Sergeant Slayback had handed him and turned his attention to his clipboard. "Now this will be approximately three and one-half minutes in length. Defense got it from an East German news service. It was shot on 5 June 1969, a little over two months ago. Location: about thirty miles north of Hanoi."

Here we go, Mary Kaye thought to herself, crossing one slacked leg over the knee of the other, isn't life groovy? A double feature! As Tony Vinza moved down the aisle, keeping his eye on the wooden tray filled with paper cups which he was carrying, she called over to him. "Hey, Tony." He hurried over to her. "Who's Miss America over there next to the brass?" She jerked her head across the aisle toward a blue-eyed Dresden doll, wearing a long-sleeved navy dress and stockings despite the heat, her hair sprayed sleekly into a short flip. The girl was flanked on one side by a trim, butch-haired Air Force colonel who must have been her father and on the other by a wrinkled but valiantly rouged mother who kept shooting worried glances across her daughter's head to her husband.

"That's Sharon Dornbeck," Sergeant Vinza explained. "Her husband punched out in June over Haiphong. Daddy's retired Air Force, an old friend of Colonel Lloyd from Norton." Sergeant Vinza's eyes flickered over to Sharon, where they stayed. She reminded him of those wholesome-faced girls with dark lipstick who sold War Bonds in the pictures gathering dust in Chester's back rooms.

"Put your eyes back in your head, Tony," Mary Kaye interrupted him. "I'm glad Casualty duty is looking up, but just remember you still have the grunts like me to take care of." Mary Kaye noticed how white Sharon's knuckles were from clutching the handle of her straw bag, and though she normally disliked fragile blond beauties as a matter of policy, she felt a twinge of sympathy for the girl.

Sergeant Vinza continued his Coke patrol. "How ya doin', Mrs. Calafano?" he asked a heavy-set woman with a gray-streaked bun, a gold cross hanging from her voluminous bosom. "How should I be doing, Tony?" she shrugged, clutching her rosary in one hand and reaching for the Coke with the other. Her husband, shriveled and silent, patted her arm, and their daughter readied the Kleenex.

"You're looking terrific in that dress," Sergeant Vinza winked at her.

Mrs. Calafano's face curled into a smile. "God bless you, Tony."

Seated a safe five rows apart from each other, Sergeant Vinza noticed the Mesdames Hochart, a mother-in-law daughter-in-law team that had not been on speaking terms since the famous Boxer Short Incident of last winter. Irma Hochart, the thin-lipped German-born mother of Master Sergeant Victor Hochart, had made a positive identification of her son from a still picture of an American prisoner with his back to the camera, wearing only a pair of boxer shorts. He was holding his elbows akimbo, apparently drinking a bowl of water or soup.

"That's Victor," she had said triumphantly to Colonel Lloyd the day she had studied "The Book" at Chester. "Those are his ears, and look how he holds the knees apart, just so."

The next day Jojo Hochart, Victor's Mississippi-bred wife of five weeks, announced that the man in the picture could not possibly be her husband. "Victor never wore boxer shorts," she observed shyly. "He wore, you know— the other kind." At this Mrs. Hochart, Sr., turned on her daughter-in-law. "For twenty-four years he lived with me. You think I don't know what kind of shorts he wears?" But Jojo stuck to her story, and the Air Force refused to make a positive identification. Now both women attended all film identification sessions, neither trusting the other.

"Clarity is fair to poor," Colonel Lloyd was continuing, "about par for the course with these films. Now once again you may freeze the film at any time—just call out a good loud 'Halt!' and we'll stop the action for you."

"Hold it for just a minute, Colonel. Sorry to interrupt." It was Tony Vinza. "I'd like to know how many people want doughnuts." The hands went up and he counted, Mary Kaye Buell, Diane Devere, the Sweringens, Margaret Holroyd, the Kubicheks, twenty-three doughnuts in all. "All set, Colonel." He gave a little wave in the direction of the stage.

"Glad to hear you're ready, Sergeant," the Colonel said with elaborate politeness. "Okay, ready up there?" The lights dimmed.

"How ya doin', honey?" Jerry Gundersen leaned over and softly asked his daughter, Sharon Dornbeck.

"I'm fine, Daddy, please don't keep askin' me."

On the screen, two North Vietnamese soldiers jogged swiftly along a jungle path, carrying a stretcher. As the stretcher passed the camera, the horizontal face turned toward the lens. At first it was blurry; then the focus cleared. . . . Slanted eyes. Only a Vietnamese. Men marching. Two Vietnamese guards patrolling back and forth in a large space which might have been part of a prison compound. A bamboo fence visible in one corner. Then a sun flare and several feet of overexposed film. An American in flight suit, cap held down at his side, stood with his back to the camera, facing his guards. The film was light and the outlines of the man seemed to blend into the grass. Suddenly he turned slightly so that his profile was briefly visible.

"Stop!"

"Hold it!" Two voices called out almost simultaneously. The frame froze.

"Daddy, that's Richard, it *is!*" Sharon Dornbeck clutched her father's arm.

"Oh, please, I think that's my husband." Carole Bogin had risen to her feet. Sandy Lawton could feel her own pulse racing. Phil Bogin had gone down a month after Roy.

The lights went on in the room, and everyone turned toward the two women who were gaping at the indistinct figure on the screen. Colonel Lloyd made it to the stage double time. "All right, we have two possible IDs," he said, "Mrs. Bogin and Mrs. Dornbeck."

Sharon, eyes straight ahead, was whispering to her father.

"The chin, Daddy, just look at the chin! It *is* Richard, can't you see?"

"It's hard to tell, honey," her father replied carefully.

Carole Bogin spoke out in a firm voice. "It looks like Phil around the chin. Sergeant Vinza." He hurried over to her. "I'd swear that's Phil's chin," she said, never taking her eyes off the screen. "But I don't know. . . . Yes, I'm pretty sure."

"Now, ladies, it's hard to establish a positive identification from that picture," Colonel Lloyd interjected smoothly. "But when the stills come in, I'll be asking both of you to come in again and bring a picture of your husbands taken from that angle, if possible. Of course, I should tell you in all fairness," he paused slightly, "this particular man has been identified by fourteen other next of kin across the country."

Carole Bogin sat down.

Colonel Lloyd cleared his throat. "In the meantime, shall we continue the film, please?"

As the lights went out again, Jerry Gundersen whispered to Sharon, "Honey, these were taken north of Hanoi, and Dick went down over Haiphong." Sharon nodded docilely and settled her hands back in her lap.

The film resumed. A basketball game. Ten emaciated prisoners, their arms flapping from pajama-like uniforms, were bouncing a ball along a mud court. Ten unknown figures with gaunt, grainy faces. Sandy Lawton's white sleeveless blouse was soaked from the fetid air in the theater. Abruptly she edged her way past Carole and Diane Devere into the aisle and walked quickly out of the darkened room.

She headed toward the car, blinded momentarily by the bright sunlight. Sergeant Vinza hurried to catch up with her. "What's the matter, Sandy? You don't want to stay?" She shook her head and continued walking. "You didn't see anyone that looked like your husband?" Tony Vinza inquired sympathetically, taking long strides so that he was even with her.

Sandy stopped and turned to Sergeant Vinza. With his deep-set brown eyes and dark curly hair, he wouldn't be bleached out in film like those ghostly figures inside, she thought. "I don't know if I did or not," she said. "There are times when I hardly remember what Roy looks like." She felt tears stinging her eyelids and was surprised to discover her sudden feeling of rage. "We were married for two weeks, and he's been missing two years! What do you people want from me!"

She turned sharply away from him toward her car. Sergeant Vinza did not follow her.

4

**Letter from Department of the Air Force to
Wife of Air Force Captain, Missing in Action**

Dear Mrs. ——————,

The following is a list of your husband's
personal effects en route to you:

3 swimming suits	Misc pictures
1 hat	& records
7 pair shorts	1 pair boots
1 athletic supporter	3 low cut shoes,
1 1505 shirt	pair
2 1505 pants	1 set cuff links
1 wallet	Misc rank
3 pair shoes	& insignia
2 Bibles	ECI chemistry course
1 belt, military	1 belt, civilian
1 alarm clock	1 Garrison hat
2 correspondence	3 ties
courses	1 Sunbeam razor

Sandy let herself into her apartment, flicked on the television, and without waiting for the image to settle, went
into her windowless kitchen and opened the refrigerator's
freezing compartment. Pulling down a cardboard container of red-white-and-blueberry ice cream, she grabbed

a large spoon and sat down in front of the TV, the carton on her lap. She wanted only to escape, to escape from the heat of Florida in August, from the Casualty Office at Chester, and from the senselessness which her life had become. She took a large spoonful of ice cream. It numbed her tongue.

". . . The Pentagon reports that casualties in Vietnam are down for the second straight month." Jesus. She flicked off the television. Still carrying the ice-cream carton, she walked aimlessly around the room, unable to decide what it was that she wanted.

"This is the kind of place you can do so much with, Mrs. Lawton," the real-estate agent had told her when he showed her the apartment. "Everything's brand spanking new, central air conditioning, dishwasher, self-cleaning oven— If you're like my wife the kitchen's the most important thing. . . ." He had rambled on. "Okay, I'll take it," Sandy had said. The agent raised his eyebrows. It was the first place he had shown her. "Yes, well, when you get a few pictures on the wall, it'll be just like home."

Now, over a year and a half later, the walls were still empty. When she left Chester, she had taken nothing but her three suitcases. It later seemed to her as if Roy had come with the furnished Air Force apartment, and when she surrendered the keys to Sergeant Vinza, she was surrendering their entire life together: apartment-complete-with-husband.

She and Alice Jacuski had gone to the Miracle Furniture Mart the week before she moved, and in an hour selected a round white formica dinette table and chairs ("extends to seat eight" but she had never used the leaves), a yellow floor-sample couch with chrome legs, two stack stools which served as end tables, a painted wooden dresser, matching black metal lamps (the protective cellophane covers were still around their shades), and a double bed. Alice had looked at her strangely when she had ordered the bed, but Alice did not understand that Sandy expected Roy back very soon.

The ice cream was getting soft. She put it away and walked into the bedroom. The bed still had no spread.

On the pillow was a fluffy blue stuffed poodle dog with glass eyes. Next to the bed a bulky rectangular shape, covered with a cheap paisley-printed cotton throw, served as her night table. On top of it were strewn two Kleenex packets, a hairbrush, a paperback Gothic romance, and in the midst of all these, a leather-framed photo of Roy Lawton, smiling under the protective steel wing of his F–4. Sandy's night table had not come from the Miracle Furniture Mart; it had been shipped by the Air Force from Udorn AFB in Thailand. When they delivered Roy's trunk over a year ago, she could not open it. For a few months it had stood upended in one corner of the bedroom, green and glaring. She could not decide what to do with it, and her indecision about the trunk seemed symptomatic to her of her indecision about what to do with her life. Finally, on an impulse, she had lowered it to rest horizontally on the floor, pushed it over next to her bed, and covered it with the maroon-and-gold throw which had been her bedspread. She knew it would have to be unpacked one day, but not yet, she told herself; in the meantime, she needed a night table.

She stared at the trunk and at the picture of Roy perched on top of it. Why did she have so much trouble remembering what he looked like, what he *really* looked like, not all official Wildroot Creme Oil and Air Force blue, but tousled in the morning or in chino pants or in his aqua bathing suit, clowning around with her in the water?

In the top drawer of her dresser, next to her stockings, was the last tape she had received from him almost two years ago. She took it out, pressed it into the portable cassette player on top of her dresser, and listened as the machine's metal and plastic insides ground out the voice of her husband in Indochina.

"Hiya, baby, how's my girl? Hey, I better not say *that* any more—" A pause in the southwestern twang— "How's my wife?" She walked over to the closet, mouthing the familiar words along with Roy. "Boy, do I miss you! Gol-ly!" Slowly, methodically, she began to take off her clothes. Navy sandals were lined up with other shoes on the fake parquet closet floor. "Been thinkin' 'bout me a little bit? 'Cuz I've sure been thinkin' 'bout you!" White blouse and navy-and-white polka dot skirt were fed into the mouth of the khaki laundry bag bulging from its brass hook. Through the slats of the Venetian blinds, the setting sun reached into the room with fingers of reddish light. "We had our R and R in Bangkok. It's a real nice town, everybody says it looks like Paris, but since I never saw Paris, I don't know. The Thai girls are supposed to be the greatest, but I wouldn't know about *that* either!" Outside, cars flashed along the highway, forsaking the breezes and pink sands of the beach for the air-conditioned clutter of Tampa. Sandy let her pants slip to the floor and stepped out of them. She unhooked her bra and hung it on the doorknob. For a moment she closed her eyes and let the air conditioning and Roy's voice wash over her firm-breasted body. Then, when she felt the prickle of goose bumps, she reached for her robe.

"Sandy?" A new voice interrupted Roy on the tape. "It's Steve. Hey, what did you do to this guy? He's the biggest party-pooper in the whole damned squadron!" Sounds of scuffling and then Roy again. "Gimme that! And haul tail before I . . ." The sound of a door slamming. Laughter from Roy and Steve.

Sandy walked over to Roy's trunk. Piling Kleenex, picture, hairbrush, and book on her bed, as Roy's Oklahoma hill voice ricocheted around the room, she pulled off the paisley cover and stared for a moment at the exposed trunk. For over a year she had dreaded opening it, dreaded the feelings that the sight of Roy's familiar things would evoke in her, and she had spared herself the task. Now, curiously calm, she began to unfasten the trunk.

"Sandy? It's me again." Roy's voice continued, high-pitched and nasal, not the way she remembered it. "I bought you a sort of long silk thing in Bangkok. Don't know where you're gonna wear it, but it's real beautiful, just like you." She stared down at his undershirts, four of them lined up across the top of the trunk. "Anyway, I hope you like it." She scooped up the T shirts one by one, carefully opened the dresser drawer, lined and reserved for

Roy, and neatly stacked the shirts in one corner. She felt nothing. Absolutely nothing. "I got your letter," he continued. "No, I never learned to play bridge. We been playin' a lot of poker here every night. It passes the time." Underpants, four pair of navy blue socks, the pale blue-and-yellow striped sport shirt she had given him because she thought it went well with his dark eyes. "When I get back you can teach me bridge and I'll teach you poker."

Underneath the shirt lay a large paper clip holding pastel money, which she opened and looked at curiously. A dreamy-eyed Oriental girl holding a basket of flowers smiled up at her against a pink paper landscape. On the other bill a solemn, mustachioed general was surrounded by curlicues of foreign language. "Man, I wish I was back with you right now." She knew the money was useless, but she tucked it neatly in the drawer anyway, under his T shirts. Why had she been dreading this for so long? One by one she scooped up Roy's safety razor and a packet of unused blades, an extra pair of navy blue shoelaces, one Ace pocket comb, and a tube of toothpaste squeezed all over. She had a fleeting, clear picture of him standing over the sink messing up the toothpaste. For a moment she felt as if a hot knife were pressing against her chest, but the feeling passed. Two ball-point pens, a worn paperback of *Catch–22,* and at the bottom of the trunk a small framed picture of a pretty, smiling girl, blond hair piled on top of her head, inscribed "To Roy, All my love forever. Sandy."

The Air Force, with total efficiency, had sent back everything that was left in Vietnam of Roy Lawton except Roy Lawton. . . .

Thud! Roy's car crashed into the back of Sandy's green mini-auto, sending it spinning across the dull metal floor. "Gotcha!" he shouted over to her as she shrieked. Jamming her foot down on the miniature brake, she gripped the wheel and yelled over to him, "Watch out, Air Force, here come the Marines!" as she bore down toward him. He pulled away and let her chase him for a while.

"Oh, help, those mean ole Marines are after me!" he piped in fake falsetto. Then, turning sharply before she could change her direction, he rammed the rubber nose of his car into the side of hers. As she careened backward, helpless and delighted, he followed, ramming her car again and again until it was pinned against the steel barrier between the Dodgems and the rest of Funorama. "Now who says the Air Force doesn't know what it's doin'?" he thundered.

"Okay, okay, I surrender!" she laughed and started to back up again. She had met him that night at a party filled with blue-suiters from Chester Air Force Base. "C'mon, Nebraska," he had whisked her toward the door, "let's go out and have some real fun!" She had followed him, not only because he was good looking in a dark-eyed, wavy-haired way, but more because he seemed, from the first moment she met him, to know exactly what he wanted. He was cocksure and impulsive.

At the amusement park, she let herself be led toward the shooting gallery. In her mind she saw him in his blue Air Force uniform, his arm draped casually, lovingly about her. She pictured him in his flight suit, coming home tired at the end of a long run. She remembered Dennis, her boy friend in North Platte, who was studying to be an engineer. When she had announced that she was planning to make her vacation in Tampa into a permanent stay, he had begged her to come back to Nebraska. "Down there's no kind of life for you, Sandy," he had pleaded with her on the phone. "I've been promised a job with the telephone company when I graduate— We could get married on what I'd be making." Her mother had called her three nights in a row. "Dennis is a wonderful boy," her mother had insisted. "You'll have a real secure life with him."

Roy was buying a turn at the shooting gallery. "Which one do you want?" he asked, indicating the prizes.

"Why don't you see how many you get and then I'll know what I can choose from?"

"That's not the way I operate. Which one?" Sandy looked at the rows of kewpie dolls, imitation Delft cups and saucers, stuffed animals, felt hats with feathers, painted Funorama pendants. "That little poodle there. The one on the middle shelf." She pointed to it, then hugged her elbows to herself, sure that Roy could not win it.

"How many do I have to get for that poodle dog there in the middle?" Roy had asked the attendant.

"Five."

"Set 'em up." Ten one-eyed ducks flipped up and moved along a plastic runway underneath the colorful honky-tonk of prizes. Roy grabbed the gun, raised it to his eyes, squinted for perfect aim, and shot down the first five pins.

He laid down the rifle. "Give her the poodle," he said to the attendant, never taking his eyes off Sandy. She felt a tingle of excitement go through her body as she took the dog and nuzzled her nose in its soft, polyester fur.

Later they sat outside around the white plastic tables of a Denny's restaurant eating hamburgers and drinking thick shakes. Sandy cuddled the little blue dog to her. "He's so sweet, Roy. I just love him."

Roy bit into his hamburger. "Yeah, well, if we get the real thing one day, it sure as hell isn't gonna be no poodle." Sandy looked up at him, startled. "I can't stand little dogs," he coninued, swallowing his hamburger, apparently unaware of what he had implied. "Irish setter's a good dog. You like Irish setters?"

She nodded. "You sure know what you want, I'll say that for you."

"Always have." He looked at her intently.

Later, as they were walking along the beach together in their bare feet, he turned to her. "You know," he said, "I'm goin' over to Vietnam pretty soon." The moon was only a sliver in the sky, and she could not see his face.

Three weeks later they were married before a justice of the peace.

They spent their honeymoon in the married officers' quarters, in a new apartment Roy had succeeded in getting just two days before the ceremony. He carried her over the threshold, and she giggled and begged to be put down. Then he turned to her, suddenly very serious. "We'll make this the best two weeks anyone ever had, baby. I don't go for this girl-in-every-port crap. As far as I'm concerned, this is it."

During the day they went to the beach, took long walks, or drove aimlessly in the white Corvair on which they blew their savings. At night, they made love. There was always a sense of urgency about it. Once Sandy said to him, "Hey, I thought in books it always took a real long time." But he just laughed and reached for her. "Why take a long time when you can do it all over again?"

At the airport, on the day he left, she gave him a leatherette-framed picture of herself and managed not to cry until the big steel bird, carrying Roy inside it, had flown off the field.

But that was over two years ago.

"Guess that's about all for now." The voice paused on the tape. "Love ya much, baby. Roy."

Sandy slammed shut the lid of the trunk and sharply pressed down the recorder's rewind button. *"Yeah,"* she screamed at the whirring machine, *"but what the hell do you look like?"* Picking up the tape, she flung it violently across the room.

5

Servicemen's Benefits for MIA/POW Families

The Department of Defense has made every effort to ensure that benefits which accrue to the families of service members are not denied to the next of kin of members missing or captured. The Department is not aware of any benefits denied because a member is missing or captured.

Moreover, there are two major benefits available to next of kin of missing or captured members which are not available to other service members and their families:

1. **Space Available Travel.**—Dependent next of kin of missing and captured personnel are authorized space available travel within the United States on military aircraft. In addition, foreign-born dependent next of kin may utilize overseas space available travel to their country of origin. (Families of members not missing or captured enjoy space available privileges overseas only when accompanied by their sponsor, or under certain emergency conditions.)

2. **Savings Program.**—A recent act of Con-

gress exempted missing and captured men and their families from the $10,000 ceiling on accruals in the Uniformed Services Savings Deposit Program. (USSDP)

—Statement by G. Warren Nutter, Assistant Secretary of Defense for International Security Affairs hearings before the Subcommittee on National Security Policy and Scientific Developments of the Committee on Foreign Affairs, House of Representatives, Ninety-first Congress

"So what's new in your young life?" Mary Kaye carried a large pile of mimeographed letters over to the dinette table, holding them in place with her chin, and dumped them in front of Sandy.

"In my life? Are you kidding?" Sandy began folding the top sheet. Slipping a letter into its envelope, she put it on the pile awaiting Diane Devere's stickered mailing lists. *Dear Congressman, You may have forgotten about our POWs and MIAs but we haven't. . . .*

"We don't have enough letters for five hundred congressmen," Sandy said, eyeing the stack.

"What the hell, most of them don't read their mail anyway." Mary Kaye sat down across from Sandy, bobby-pinned her long loose hair behind her ears, and set to work.

"Then what are we sending them for?"

"My dear girl, I have three years' worth of letters from the Casualty office instructing me never, repeat *never* to reveal to anyone outside of my immediate family that Brian is a POW. Now that they've finally unmuzzled us, I'll be goddamned if I'm not going to at least *try* to get the news out. If people don't know what's happening, it won't be *our* fault." Mary Kaye grinned saucily. "Besides, like what else do we have to do with our evenings?"

"Amen to that," Sandy sighed.

Sometimes Sandy looked just like a child, Mary Kaye thought, especially now, barefoot, one tanned leg tucked under pale pink shorts, her forehead furrowed as she carefully creased each letter into thirds. Just as war bound together the men under fire, Mary Kaye thought, it united the women left behind back home.

She and Sandy had met a year earlier when Sandy accidentally overheard Mary Kaye administer a tongue-lashing to Colonel Lloyd.

"Now look, you fellas want me to include three mysterious lines in my next letter to my husband. I have a right to know what they mean." The voice coming out of Lloyd's office was high and lilting, but the audacity of the speaker stunned Sandy, who was sitting in the outer office listening through the half-open door.

"Mrs. Buell, that information is classified." Colonel Lloyd sounded uneasy; he wasn't used to challenges, especially from women. "When you *need to know*," he bristled, "rest assured we'll tell you." There was a pause in the conversation, and Sandy wondered how the woman inside was taking the rebuke. "By the way," Colonel Lloyd continued, "Randolph called this morning. It seems you haven't been forwarding Captain Buell's letters for Intelligence to examine."

"That's right. Tell you how it is, Colonel Lloyd. Those letters are addressed to me, right?"

"Yes, but . . ."

"And when there's anything in them you people *need to know* you can rest assured I'll send them along." With that, the speaker marched out of Lloyd's office, her brown pony tail swinging behind her. She took a rumpled raincoat from the chair next to Sandy and said, "He's all yours."

"Who was that woman, Colonel Lloyd?" Sandy asked later. And she had looked up Mary Kaye's number in the phone book, called her although she didn't know quite why, and was the immediate recipient of an invitation for a pot-luck dinner. They saw each other frequently after that, and if their relationship verged on that of mother and daughter, this displeased neither of them. Sandy welcomed Mary Kaye's tough-minded, pragmatic approach.

"Did I tell ya what happened right after Bri went down?" Mary Kaye gave up on symmetrical folds and shoved the letters in the envelopes any which way they fit. "I called the Air Force to find out when Brian's paycheck would come so I could pay for groceries, little things like that? And they said, 'Mrs. Buell, we're going to hold his pay in escrow until we verify that he didn't go AWOL.' So I said, 'Fellas, my husband may be dumb enough to be a career officer in the Air Force but he is *not* dumb enough to go AWOL over North Vietnam!'"

Sandy was still laughing when Julie came wandering into the kitchen, two buttons pinned to her T shirt. One read, YOU'RE A GOOD MAN, CHARLIE BROWN, the other, HAVE A HEART, HANOI.

"What's funny?" she asked.

"Your mother!" Sandy scooped the child into her lap. "Want me to fix your hair?" Julie nodded, and Sandy undid the two red barrettes behind the little girl's ears and let her hair hang loose for a minute. "You know something, Julie Buell?" She stroked the child's long chestnut hair. "You're gonna knock 'em dead when you grow up."

"Will you make bunches?" Julie asked.

Sandy separated her hair into two clumps, snapping first one barrette and then the other into place. "There you go."

Mary Kaye watched her daughter slide off Sandy's lap and run to preen in the hall mirror. At least, Mary Kaye thought to herself, she had the children. They imposed a certain order on her life. They were "ongoing"—that was the only word for it; they didn't stop, and if you were their mother, neither could you.

"Sandy, did you call Walton State?"

"Not yet." Sandy began licking envelopes. The gum tasted slick and unpleasant.

"What are you waiting for? You gotta go back to school. It's the only thing that kept me from going bananas, finishing my degree and starting to teach. At least if you're doing something interesting during the days, the nights aren't so bad."

"It's one thing for you. You know Brian is a prisoner.

Okay, you haven't got him here, but you know he's in North Vietnam, and you get letters. . . ."

"Such as they are."

"Yeah, but you get them. Every month I write a letter to Lt. Roy Lawton, c/o the Democratic Republic of Vietnam, no address, nothing. It's like sending it out into a great void. I feel so peculiar every time I put one in the mailbox, writing to someone who might be alive and then again just might be dead."

"Sandy, when Brian went down, I said to myself, he's in prison, that's his problem. I'm here, that's mine. You gotta make a life for yourself."

"Okay, here's another thing. Let's say I quit my job and go back to school. What if they change Roy's status from missing to killed? I'd get zilch from the Air Force. What would I live on?"

Mary Kaye folded her arms and glared. "What are you saving all his paychecks for, the house you and Roy are gonna have *in case* they find him, *in case* he comes back?"

"Okay! I'm gonna call Walton, I just haven't got around to it yet." Sandy took the pile of completed envelopes and lined them up neatly in a carton.

Mary Kaye watched for a moment, a provocative glint in her eye. "You gotta look for the silver lining. Like my mother. She thinks I have the perfect setup—the children, the house, all of Brian's paychecks and I don't even have to sleep with him!"

Sandy laughed. "Maybe she's right, I don't know," Mary Kaye continued. "I don't miss sex all that much— It's more the companionship, know what I mean?" She paused and looked at Sandy.

"Mmm." Sandy avoided Mary Kaye's eyes. She had never thought of Roy as a companion. It seemed to her a strange word, something to do with old people. Perhaps companionship developed later in a marriage.

The next month, Sandy enrolled at Walton State College, an educational institution that was strictly Florida Modern: pastel-stucco and glass buildings, façades punctuated at decent intervals by bougainvillaea, lawns raped of trees and assuaged by sun-kissed carpet grass, the whole complex looking as if it were hothouse-grown overnight, blandly attractive, not too lush to be distracting. Twenty minutes from Tampa and near the beach, Walton State drew local would-be teachers and out-of-staters who failed to get into colleges of their choice or were lured by Walton's endless summer of education.

Sandy walked along the concrete paths, trying to find the book co-op. She wore medium-heeled white pumps and a brown-and-white tweed short-sleeved dress with a white linen Peter Pan collar. (In North Platte the first day at school was always an occasion to dress up.) At Walton State boys in tattered Levi shorts, barefoot and tanned, and girls with long swinging hair, tight-thighed bell-bottoms, and soundless moccasins glided past her, relaxed, casual, sure of where they were going. She felt out of place, nervous, vastly older and less self-confident than the bronzed students around her. At Walton State Sandy was anonymous, a number in the registrar's office. She thought fleetingly of Alice at the bank, on her coffee break by now.

Her heels clicking against the concrete sounded loud and jarring, as she walked up to a girl in a loose-fitting Indian cotton shift, adorned with tiny mirrors. "Excuse me, could you tell me where the book co-op is?"

"Right over there." The girl pointed to a small red-brick building off to the left.

"Thanks." Sandy smiled and started toward it.

"Oh, Miss?" the girl called. Sandy turned around, startled at the deference. "It's in the basement." The girl smiled politely.

Entering the building, Sandy made her way down the marble stairs and through the turnstile into the bustle of students buying first-semester supplies. She snapped open her thick three-ring notebook and pulled out her reading list, noticing with a sidelong glance that most of the other students used spiral-bound, hardcover notebooks, a separate one for each course.

She moved through the stacks to the section labeled Poli. Sci. and began taking down the books she needed.

Problems of American Political History by Grossbart was on the top shelf above her head, and she could not reach it. Next to her, a tall, bushy-haired young man was intently leafing through a book, *Hell in a Very Small Place*, by Bernard Fall. Sandy noticed the title more than the young man. Another author she had never heard of. "Hey, excuse me. Could you reach that book up there for me?"

"Sure." He quickly put his own book back in the stacks and reached up to where she was pointing. She didn't know why, but she had the impression that he had been noticing her even before she spoke. "Which one?"

"That's it," she said, as his hand closed around Grossbart. "Boy, you sure have to be tall around here."

"There's a stepladder right at the end there." He handed her the book and smiled slightly from somewhere above his coppery beard.

"Oh. Right. Thanks." She glanced over at the stepladder, feeling foolish.

"It's all right. I didn't mind getting it for you." He seemed embarrassed, as if she might have thought he hadn't wanted to help her. He was wearing sneakers and khaki wash pants. The color of Roy's fatigues. On his faded blue denim shirt, he wore a peace button. "Need any more help?"

"No, thanks." Sandy checked off Grossbart and turned to the next course on her reading list. She sensed rather than saw that he had turned his attention back to the stacks. "Are the ed books around here?" she asked him.

"On the other side. I'll show you." He headed around the bookstacks, and she noticed how the back of his brown hair curled over the collar of his shirt. The thought flashed through her mind that she had never before talked, really talked, to anybody with long hair.

"What are you taking in ed?" he asked her.

"Early Childhood Education."

"Yes? With Webber?"

"No. Hailey." She hesitated, but he seemed interested. "I'm majoring in ed. I want to teach first grade, I think."

He studied the list in her hand. "You look like you'd be

a good first-grade teacher," he said, beginning to take books down for her.

"Why?" she asked, suddenly curious at how she must appear to him. "What does a good first-grade teacher look like?"

"Oh, I don't know." He glanced over at her, not quite meeting her eyes. "Cheerful."

"Me? Cheerful?" Sandy began to laugh.

"You don't like that?" He seemed upset; in some way he had displeased her. "Listen," he said, taking a paperback down from the stacks. "Hailey doesn't assign this, but if you're really interested in young children, you should read it."

Sandy looked over at the book he was holding. "Pia-get?" she said, mispronouncing the name.

"Piaget," he corrected her. "Rhymes with 'sway.' Webber always assigns him."

She took the book and placed it on top of the pile in her arms. "Say, is this Webber a lot better than Hailey?"

"Well." He shifted his weight onto his other foot and stroked his beard. "He's about thirty years younger and, nine out of ten students feel, far more handsome." He looked down at her, and she noticed the twinkle of his blue eyes behind the steel-rimmed spectacles.

"Hey," Sandy looked at him teasingly, "Webber wouldn't by any chance have a beard and wear granny glasses, would he?"

He grinned. "Alan Webber. You're? . . ."

"Sandy Lawton." She was smiling broadly now.

"Hi." They stood looking at each other, and neither of them could think of anything further to say. "Well, I guess that's it." Sandy shifted her arms to get a better grip on her books. "Thanks for all your help."

"That's okay." Alan watched her go over to the cashier and stand in line. Her legs were slim, and the curves of her figure in the fitted dress were trimly restrained. The kind of girls he knew never wore fitted waistlines; they wore hip-huggers with their boy friends' shirts hung low-bellied over them or knotted at the midriff. He watched Sandy head up the marble stairs and out the door and decided that she was exactly the kind of girl who would never be attracted to him. She was created to go out with football heroes and identify with Pepsi-generation ads. He turned back to his books. Then on impulse he bounded through the turnstile, up the steps out of the book co-op.

"Hey," he said, catching up with her. "You probably need help carrying those."

"Oh, no, thanks. I can manage."

They stood awkwardly in front of the door. "You got time for a cup of coffee maybe?"

She grabbed her books more tightly. "Oh, no, no. I couldn't possibly. I have to go now," and she started to walk away from him. He felt that in some way he had scared her.

A few steps away, she stopped, somehow sensing that he had taken her panic for a rebuff, and looked back at him. Standing there, he reminded her of a great shaggy bear, awkward and friendly, menacing only if he moved toward you too fast. "On second thought," she said, her voice overly bright, "where do you go for a cup of coffee around here?"

They were seated around a beige-and-white-flecked formica table at The Hole in the Wall, Walton State's coffee shop in the back of its theater arts building. Sandy sipped a steaming mug of black coffee and looked past Alan at the students sprawled on counter stools, book bags draped casually over their shoulders, smoking cigarettes and catching up on a summer of news. Everyone seemed to know everyone else.

"Do you teach anything besides Early Childhood Ed?" she asked Alan.

"That's all. The rest of the time I'm supposed to spend in the library writing the great work of our century—my thesis."

"What's it about?" she asked.

"Let me see"—he looked up at the ceiling—"I keep forgetting. Last time I looked it dealt with the effects of Caleb Gattegno's reading theory on slow learners." He buttered an English muffin with both pats of butter from the cardboard container. "Now isn't that something you'd want to rush out and read?"

"Why do you make fun of yourself?" she asked him ingenuously. "I'll bet it *is* interesting."

Alan looked at her curiously. She didn't seem to know that cynicism was fashionable.

"Hey, wouldn't you know it?" He reached over and picked up her left hand, looking down at her wedding ring. "Where's Mr. Lawton?"

Sandy's heart began to race. She took her hand away and put it in her lap. "Vietnam."

Alan looked at her, now genuinely curious. Everyone he knew was either a conscientious objector or had managed to get a student deferment. "Vietnam? When's he due back?"

Sandy put her hands around the hot coffee mug and watched the steam curl up from it. "I don't know. He's been missing in action since October 14, 1967." She realized that she had never had to tell that to anyone before. In her past life, the life she had led up until yesterday, everyone knew about her. There were no explanations, no dread of the moment when people would look at her differently. *Would* they look at her differently? She glanced up at him.

His face held genuine sympathy. "I'm sorry." His blue eyes, inside the fuzzy brown halo of hair, were kind. It occurred to her that despite his long hair and sophistication about books, he was shy. She nodded; it was all right.

"Gee, that's really rough. Almost two years."

"One year, eleven months and ten days, but who's counting?" Sandy answered brightly.

He took a bite out of his muffin and they both sipped their coffee. Next to them a girl with long frizzy red hair, in tie-dyed polo shirt and jeans, leaned over toward her date, wiggling a cigarette between her teeth. He bent forward, a lean, sun-tanned jock, and ignited her cigarette from his own, laughing as she blew smoke in his face.

"Do you go out?" Alan was speaking to her. The question sounded casual.

"You mean date? Of course not." She grabbed her mug and took another swallow of coffee. It was lukewarm by now.

"Why 'of course not'?"

Sandy put down the coffee and stared at Alan incredulously. "Well—that's just— I mean—" she found herself spluttering. "That's just the way I feel about it, that's all!"

"Okay, sorry. You know," he added, "in India women throw themselves on their husbands' funeral pyres."

Sandy stood up, suddenly angry, at Alan for talking to her this way, at herself for being in the coffee shop with him. "Look," she said, "I don't even know you!" She gathered up her books, annoyed to find her hands trembling, and hurried to the door.

As she headed toward the parking lot, Alan caught up with her. "Sandy." He grabbed her elbow and forced her to look at him. "I didn't meant to upset you." She said nothing, only waited for him to finish so she could run—away from him, away from her first day at Walton. "It's just that some women like playing the martyred wife." He looked at her placatingly.

She jerked her elbow away and with an intensity she did not know she possessed almost spat out at him, "Well, I don't! I *hate* it!"

6

**Air Force Directive to Next of Kin:
Prisoner Correspondence**

We recommend that letters be of a cheerful
nature and be confined to personal and family
matters. Write about activities of family and
friends, such as vacations, visits, schooling,
and other events and comments of interest.
Suggest that no mention be made regarding
the current status or pros and cons of the
conflict in Southeast Asia, victories or losses
of our military forces, other service personnel who are MIA or captured, etc. In
short, comments either closely or remotely
connected with the current political or military situation in Southeast Asia should be
avoided. Letters should be directed at bracing
the PW's morale and should not contain
information which can be used by his
captors. Because personal handwriting is
often difficult for people of other nation-
alities to read, we feel that letters limited
to one page, typewritten or clearly printed,
have a better chance of getting through to
our PWs. Please retain a copy of every
letter you forward as it may become necessary for us to refer to them at a later date.

In October of 1969, Sandy decided she had to take some direct action to try to find out if Roy was alive or dead. For two years she had been content to sit back and wait for the Air Force to find him, placidly hoping that the machinery called government would grind along in its unfathomable way and deliver her husband to her. She had followed Air Force rules about not speaking to the press, had dutifully pored over photographs and regularly squinted at blurry films. She had responded to all the proddings and suggestions of Pentagon, Air Force, and State. Now she decided she could no longer remain passive.

The fourteenth of the month marked the second anniversary of Roy's being shot down. The most memorable feature of the day was that it went by totally unmarked. She had taken a Psychology 100 quiz in the morning. ("If a rat wants a pellet of food but, every time he takes the pellet, receives an electric shock, that is called a ___?___ ." "Double bind," she had written.)

She went home and checked her mailbox. No word from the Air Force, the Pentagon, or even her own parents, who were scrupulous about events like birthdays, graduations, and wedding anniversaries but who, after all, had no reason to remember the date that their son-in-law, whom they had never met, went to his death or captivity—which?—in North Vietnam.

In the evening, Sandy put through a call to Roy's parents in their trailer camp in Oklahoma. They were out. She heated up a can of Spaghetti-O's, and stared blankly at her books. The lack of definition was what bothered her most, more even than the loneliness. She was neither wife nor widow; she could not plan her life with Roy, or without him. Her days seemed devoid of the usual markers of grief or hope: there was nothing to look forward to, nor anything to mourn the passing of. And no end to this emotional wasteland was in sight.

Walton State might have marked the beginning of a new life for her, yet she was unable to enter into it fully. She was not like the other students, for whom classes marked the time between beach and a beer. Aside from a nodding acquaintance with the people on her right and left in the large lectures she attended, Sandy had made no friends at Walton. In military circles she was statusless; at college, she remained anonymous. (One of her classes was given on closed-circuit television: she would file into a large hall, sit down and focus her attention first on a test pattern, then shifting gray-and-white lines, then at last on a balding black-and-white face.)

Sandy thought back to the second time she had seen Alan Webber, a few days ago. He had told her she was wasting her life, and perhaps he was right. She had looked up and found him smiling down over her shoulder in the library. "How do you like Hailey?" he asked her in a low voice. She smiled back at him. "You're right," she whispered, "Webber would have been better." He motioned for her to follow him outdoors.

They perched on a low wall, watching the fountain in the center of the courtyard and the students walking past it. "Hey, about the other day," Alan looked over at her, "I'm sorry."

"Oh, that's okay." She glanced at a slender brunette walking toward the library dressed in skintight blue jeans and a loose embroidered peasant blouse. "Guess I'll have to invest in a pair of Levis if I'm going to stay here."

"Yeah," Alan said, watching the brunette, "you'd look good in tight Levis." Sandy smiled, embarrassed at the flattery. "Hey," he turned to her, "do you mind telling me how come you got so ticked off at me the other day?"

"I didn't get ticked off," she protested. "It's just that I get so sick and tired of discussing my 'situation' all the time. It's like I can't get away from it. That's all anybody wants to talk about, you included."

Alan's blue eyes looked directly into her own. "I'd like to talk about lots of other things with you. . . ."

Sandy stood up to leave. "Hey, wait a minute." He grabbed her notebook, fumbled in his pocket for a ballpoint pen, and wrote his telephone number on the slate-blue cover. "If you ever decide to come out of that hermetically sealed vacuum you call your life, give me a ring.

I'd like to take you to a movie or something. I won't even hold your hand—I promise."

Sandy grabbed the notebook and headed back to the library. Behind her she heard Alan saying, "Sandy, will you call me?" She kept on walking. "Don't hold my breath, huh?"

She *had* to find out if Roy was alive or dead. She was twenty-one years old. The uncertainty was unbearable.

The next Thursday Sandy attended a meeting of POW/MIA families in the Tampa area, held in the home of Margaret Holroyd. Margaret was the thirty-year-old wife of POW John Holroyd, fortunate enough to be confined in the "luxury" prison camp known as the Hanoi Hilton. Margaret, too, was fortunate. Every Christmas she watched her husband playing volleyball on the Walter Cronkite show in a film clip which did exactly what the North Vietnamese intended: confused the American public. The few prisoners who had escaped bore tales of atrocities, but these smiling, ball-throwing men looked fit and well fed, like suburban fathers having a Sunday game in the park. Were the rest of the prisoners being treated equally well, or were they being tortured? The families of the prisoners, and the American public, never knew for sure.

Mary Kaye Buell, sprawled on the carpet in Margaret's living room, watched the women settle themselves on the couches and borrowed bridge chairs and reflected that this was one organization where membership growth was no problem.

Though this was only the third meeting of the Tampa group, Mary Kaye felt its formation marked the beginning of the end of the POW wives' long adolescence under the government's paternal hand. For five years, since the first flier was downed in 1964, the government had urged POW and MIA next of kin to avoid publicity, keep a low profile, and let Washington handle everything, and for five years the women had played by the government's rules. In return, they had received only a trickle of mail and almost no information about their men. So much for Washington, Mary Kaye thought. She had been one of the founders of the Tampa group and had been gratified to discover that next-of-kin groups were springing up in other parts of the country. There were POW/MIA families in all fifty states by now and there was even talk of forming a national organization.

The Tampa group's long-range goal was, of course, to bring the men home. In the meantime, they pressed for more immediate results, such as hard information about which of their men designated as Missing in Action were, in fact, alive; better treatment of prisoners; improvement in the flow of mail. But, Mary Kaye was realistic enough to know, the group's most important function was to give its member families, for whom the American dream was interrupted by the effrontery of Indochina, a sense of community and purpose.

"When's it due?" Mary Kaye reached up from the floor and patted Diane Devere's stomach.

"November," Diane said, looking up from her knitting. She was a sallow girl, thin, except for the bulge of her stomach. Mary Kaye watched her biting her lower lip as she knit. Diane's husband was lost over Laos, which was like being jettisoned in outer space: the Pathet Lao had never acknowledged the existence of a single American flier.

"You hoping for a boy?" Mary Kaye asked her.

"I don't much care." Diane shrugged and continued knitting.

Margaret Holroyd only hoped she had enough coffeecake to go around. The recipe had said "feeds six" and she had doubled it, but there must be fifteen in the room by now. She placed the aqua cut-glass plate filled with cake (sliced extra thin) on the coffee table next to the Oreos and the forty-cup electric urn. "Just help yourselves, everyone," she smiled out at the group. "Food, pamphlets, whatever you need, just make yourselves at home." Margaret had been an airline stewardess before she met John, and as Mary Kaye, who adored her, thought, the TWA training had stuck. Margaret was professionally cheerful and unruffled by disaster.

"I think we'd better begin now." Margaret settled herself in a flower-covered wing chair. "First I want to formally welcome Sharon Dornbeck, the newest member of the club nobody wants to join." Margaret turned to smile at Sharon, who was seated primly on a bridge chair, knees together, hands folded in her lap. "Just to fill you in, Sharon, most of our husbands—or sons—" she glanced apologetically at Mrs. Calafano— "are missing in action. I think just three of us—yes, Mary Kaye, Mrs. Kubichek and me—have heard from our men in POW camps."

"Excuse me," Mrs. Kubichek broke in. "I want to clarify a point. Actually I don't get the letters, my daugher-in-law does, because she's primary next of kin, and I'm only secondary."

Mary Kaye locked her arms behind her head and looked at the ceiling. Jane York pulled out crocheting. "Yes, Mrs. Kubichek," Margaret tried to break in.

"And she's all the way out in Denver," Mrs. Kubichek continued, looking at Sharon and twisting a handkerchief in her puffy fingers. "It's funny, I'm his mother, I raised him, but I'm only secondary."

"Mrs. Kubichek, I think that we'd better move on," Margaret suggested sweetly.

"I'm just mentioning it." Mrs. Kubichek pursed her lips, crumpled the handkerchief into a ball, and shifted so that the other half of her enormous Banlon-covered weight would get some support in the narrow bridge chair.

"Now," Margaret glanced down at the clipboard on her lap, "Mrs. Calafano, how're you coming along with the bumper stickers? Are they back from the printer yet?"

"Next Monday they'll be ready. Vincent's gonna get them, then I'll bring them over and we can all take our quota."

"Good," Margaret nodded encouragingly, "and please, everybody, be sure to pick them up. It's important that we each do our part distributing them. Mary Kaye, how's the mailing campaign coming along?"

"Sandy and I sent letters to every congressman," Mary Kaye explained, "urging that they take a public stand on the prisoner issue and demand North Vietnamese compliance with the Geneva Convention. So far we have had exactly two replies, which brings up the really scary question: how many of our elected representatives know how to read?"

Jojo Hochart turned her head away, as if to avoid contamination from Mary Kaye's disaffection.

"Excuse me." Sandy sat forward in her bridge chair, speaking softly. "I've got to say something. I think we're all just wasting our time." Diane Devere put down her knitting, and Mary Kaye looked at her friend, startled. "I mean, I think it's fine to put bumper stickers on cars and write to congressmen and all that, but, well, that doesn't help most of us find out what we really want to know. I know it doesn't tell me what I want to know." Her voice was insistent now. "Is my husband alive or dead?" She saw Jane York nodding. "I'm tired of waiting to hear from congressmen, waiting to hear from the Pentagon, waiting to hear from everyone. I don't know how all of you feel, but I know I've got to *do* something! I've decided I'm going to go to Páris. I'm going to go to the North Vietnamese delegation and I'm going to ask them: is he alive? Am I a wife or a widow?"

"The North Vietnamese!" Sharon Dornbeck's voice expressed her shock. "You aren't gonna talk to *them?*"

"I'm sure Sandy'd rather talk to the Italians or the British," Mary Kaye said acidly, "but unfortunately our husbands went down over North Vietnam. Good for you, San!" She turned to her friend. "When are you going?"

"Over Thanksgiving vacation," Sandy said, "and I'd love any other MIA wife here to come along with me." She looked around the room.

"But why should they tell you anything?" Sharon asked, wrinkling her forehead in dismay.

"I hope you're not planning to use any funds from the kitty," Mrs. Kubichek interjected.

"No, Mrs. Kubichek." Sandy sighed. "I'm going on my own money, and, Sharon, I don't know if they'll tell me anything. I only know I can't sit around here any more and just wait. I think maybe if I go, maybe if a few of us go—and if we look them in the eye and ask them if our husbands are alive—they might just tell us. Anyway, we're never going to find out anything sitting *here!*"

"I feel it is important," Jojo Hochart spoke up in her Mississippi drawl, "that Sandy make it clear she is representin' herself only and not the Tampa group. I personally don't see the point of fussin' and protestin' and demandin' to see the enemy, like a bunch of crazy students or leftists or somethin'. I don't want my name in any way connected with this. My husband's a career officer."

"You know, Sandy," Diane Devere said placatingly, "my mother always used to say you catch more flies with honey than with vinegar."

"Well, my mother used to say the wheel that squeaks gets the grease," Sandy retorted.

"I have an idea," Mary Kaye said drily, "let's send our mothers over."

Cake, Margaret thought, just the thing to pacify everyone.

"I just want to say," Mrs. Calafano spoke, taking two slices of the thinly cut cake in her fat fingers, "that I have no intention of going to Paris. Vincent and I still believe in our government." She eyed Sandy suspiciously as she bit into the cake. "Mmm, Margaret," she said, crumbs flying over her shiny black dress, "this is delicious!"

Margaret beamed. "Isn't it? I cut the recipe out of the paper. It's called 'Easy Coffee Cake.' "

"You have the recipe handy? I'd like to copy it."

"I'll go with you, Sandy." Jane York spoke up quietly. "I got the money saved up, and anyway," she smiled, "you can probably use me. They can't very well refuse to see another member of the Third World!" Sandy laughed. Jane, the only black member of the group, had been forced off the base when her husband, an Air Force captain, went down two years ago, and she was now living in the black section of Tampa.

"Great! Anyone else care to come?" Sandy looked around.

"When are you goin' again?" Sharon asked.

Sandy was surprised. "Over Thanksgiving. Why don't you come?"

Sharon was clasping and unclasping her hands around the black leather handle of her pocketbook. "Well, I don't know. I've got to talk it over with my dad—he's retired Air Force. . . ."

"It might be a no-no?" Mary Kaye asked sweetly.

Sharon glowered at her, needled by the sarcasm and the suspicion that Mary Kaye might just be right.

7

Contacts with News Media

The decision to talk to a news media representative is one each next of kin must make in light of his or her own convictions. . . . We cannot tell the next of kin what to say to the news media, nor what not to say. The following is offered only as advice. . . .

It is suggested that the best way to handle the interview is to use a humanitarian approach, e.g., my children and I are required to bear additional anxieties because the enemy refuses to release welfare information concerning my husband; this is in violation of the Geneva Convention. Further, it would be in your best interest not to discuss the situation in terms of national policy or politics as relates to our involvement in Southeast Asia. The rationale for this recommendation is that policy and politics are not germane to the disregard of the Geneva Convention by the enemy.

—Directive to Next of Kin,
from Randolph Air Force Base

Sharon Dornbeck's room in her parents' house had not been redone when she got married. The Gundersens never made it into a guest room, as so many of their friends had done with the bedrooms of married offspring, because the Gundersens never really believed their only child had left. Just as some women are thought of primarily as mothers, and some seem to the outside world wives first and foremost, Sharon was, above all, a daughter.

Her parents were both from old Florida families. Paula Gundersen's inheritance from her father's lumberyards purchased, early in Jerry's career, the kind of security that most military families never know: a large, Georgian brick house on a tree-shaded patch of land. As Jerry Gundersen moved up in the military, Paula and Sharon followed him when necessary, once on a two-year stint to Washington, and once to Norton in California; but the solidly built Tampa house, though occasionally rented out, was always home. The house revolved around Jerry, and even now that her husband was retired and home all the time, Paula Gundersen still showered every afternoon punctually at four-thirty, a habit ingrained from years of "freshening up" for the arrival of the head of the house.

Paula was a petite woman with regular features, who still had her hair set in flat finger waves because she felt that roller height was too ostentatious. Though overshadowed in almost every way by the other two members of her family—Jerry was far more assertive and Sharon light-years prettier—Paula never objected. She seemed to exist only through her relationships to others. Her roles were to provide an obliging, on-time, well-decorated background for her husband, to ease her daughter past the shoals of growing up, and now to extend her always-available services to her grandson. She was a soothing presence, who demanded little for herself. Even her one hobby, gardening, was engaged in more to please her husband and daughter with cut flowers than for any intrinsic love of horticulture.

Sharon was the pluperfect daughter, obedient to her parents' wishes, even to the innocent genetic fluke of being more beautiful than they had hoped. At Florida State, she

was sorority queen and later Homecoming Queen (Paula
Gundersen still kept the clippings in the piano bench),
and upon graduation, had married a broad-shouldered Air
Force Academy graduate with what promised to be a
brilliant future. Richard Dornbeck, her father was pleased
to see, treated Sharon with the protectiveness Jerry knew
she needed. "Princess," her father called his daughter, upon
occasion treating her like a Spanish infanta, frozen in time,
and surrounding her with whatever royal trappings he
could provide.

When Sharon's husband Richard was sent to Indochina,
it seemed by far the most sensible plan for Sharon to move
back in with her parents, particularly since they would
help her take care of her son, Ricky, then only three. Some
days, back in her old bedroom, she felt as if she were a
young girl again. The room supported her illusion. She
slept in her childhood four-poster bed with its white dotted-
Swiss canopy and dust ruffle. Opposite it were a French
provincial dresser, painted pink and white, and a white
rocker with pink gingham cushions. The bookshelves held
a mixed assortment of *Heidi,* Nancy Drew mysteries, *Forever Amber,* and Sharon's doll collection, featuring dolls
culled from her father's military hops, though the place of
honor was still occupied by Raggedy Ann.

When Richard punched out, of course there was no
question but that Sharon would stay on with her parents.
She needed them, and they were ready to be needed. When,
a month after Richard went down, it came time to buy
Ricky's school clothes and arrange his fifth birthday party,
it was Paula Gundersen who undertook both tasks, allowing Sharon as much depressed sleep as she craved. Jerry
Gundersen used all his military connections, which were
not inconsiderable, to try to gain more information for his
daughter about her husband's fate. Sharon obeyed her
father—more than that, she relied on him—but all the
time she was living in this extended family, she had the
nagging feeling that there was something she had been
meaning to do and she couldn't quite remember what it
was.

She knew her father would be upset when she broached the subject of going to Paris with Sandy and Jane.

"You think the North Vietnamese are goin' to give you some information about Richard?" Jerry Gundersen, seated in the chintz armchair, puffing on his pipe, looked at her skeptically. "No way. You're just plain naïve, Sharon."

"But, Daddy . . ."

"For God's sake," he thundered, "we're fightin' a war against 'em!" His voice softened as he saw his daughter's distress. "Sharon, how do you think this would look for Dick's career? Do you think he'd want you to do this?"

"I don't know, Daddy." She still had this nagging feeling at the back of her mind.

"Princess," he looked at her kindly, thinking what a damned shame it was that she should be going through this, "don't you trust me?" Sharon looked at her father, nodding, and Jerry could see the tears in her eyes. "I've never steered you wrong, have I? I spent twenty years of my life in the Air Force, and I'm here to tell you that the boys in the Pentagon aren't sittin' around twiddlin' their thumbs. If there's information to be got, they'll get it for you. Give your own people a chance!"

"But, Daddy, it's been more than two years for Sandy and Jane York, and they haven't heard a *word!*"

Jerry put down his pipe. "And they don't have fathers who can pick up the phone and get in touch with anybody they please right up to the Under Secretary of Defense, either! Sharon, I called Ev Holmquist in Saigon! You were here, you heard me!"

"Daddy, I know. I know you're lookin' out for me, and I appreciate it." She took a deep breath. "But I'm a married woman now, and I have to do what I think is best. I'm goin' to Paris."

She looked at her father's astonished face and was suddenly aware that the nagging feeling in her head had stopped.

The night she was packing to leave, Ricky wandered into the room. He stood watching her put her clothes into the blue airplane suitcase. "Why do you have to go, Mommy?"

"Ricky, I've told you three times." Sharon looked up from the apricot silk robe she was folding. "I'm going to Paris to see a man about Daddy."

The little boy wound his arms and legs around a poster of the bed. "Are you going to bring Daddy home?"

"No, darlin'. I'm goin' to ask the man to tell me about Daddy."

"Are you gonna bring the man home?" Ricky had unwound himself from the bed post and was opening his mother's jars of cold cream and toilet water on top of the dresser.

"No. Don't play with those, Ricky. They'll break." Sharon slipped black lace panties, bra, and petticoat neatly into the zippered underwear compartment. Ricky was by now smearing a dab of Etherea cold cream on his hands and rubbing it in. "Sweetheart, why don't you go down and ask Grandma to give you a treat?"

Ricky looked up at his mother and continued to rub the cold cream into his hand. "Mommy, is Daddy dead?"

Sharon dropped the white blouse she had been holding on top of the other clothes in her suitcase. She picked up Ricky and sat him down on her lap in the pink-and-white rocker. "Daddy is not dead." She turned the child to face her. "Ricky, do you understand?" The boy nodded, his eyes wide. "But some bad men are keepin' him in their country and they won't tell us where. I'm goin' to ask the man in Paris if he can find out."

The child gripped the side of the rocker, while bouncing on his mother's knee. "And then we'll get a gun and shoot the bad men and we'll go get Daddy! Is Daddy coming home in an airplane?"

Sharon sighed. "Yes, when Daddy comes home, he'll come in an airplane."

"Ricky!" Sharon's mother called up the stairs. "C'mon down here and don't bother your mama." The boy slid off his mother's lap and ran down to his grandmother. Sharon returned to her packing.

The one thing Jerry Gundersen did do when he realized his daughter was actually defying him and going to Paris was to insist that she and Sandy and Jane at least talk with General Fletcher Gibbs of the Pentagon. Gibby, as he was known to his intimates (and Jerry Gundersen was one of his intimates, having fought a desk war with him in Korea) was the top Pentagon man in charge of POW families. State assigned an FSO-2 to deal with the families, and the Pentagon gave the job to a full general, tacit recognition of the fact that the next of kin could be a sticky problem. If their situation could not be solved by Washington, at least high-level people should be seen dealing with it.

Gibby was delighted to talk with the women. While Jerry Gundersen felt that it was a waste of time for his daughter to go to Paris, strangely enough the Pentagon did not. Although the official military position on all matters regarding PNOK (primary next of kin) was that what the families did was their own business, in reality the Pentagon tried to suggest proper behavior at every step of the way. While the women were of course free to write whatever they wanted to their husbands, the Pentagon suggested certain topics deemed to be of a "cheerful nature"; while the women were of course free to talk to whatever media people they wished, the Pentagon mailed out suggested procedures for what to say; and while a PNOK trip to Paris was of course a private matter, Fletcher Gibbs was only too happy to brief the women beforehand, set up any meetings he could, and certainly debrief them later. After all, there was always the outside chance that a few defenseless women would be able to learn something their government couldn't.

In fact, Gibby had even put the Tampa contingent in touch with two other MIA next of kin who had told the Pentagon they wanted to go to Paris. Now five women were facing him in his office, properly blinded by the military dazzle: Fay Clausen, wife of a Navy commander from San Diego, Mrs. Doyle, mother of an Army corporal from Indiana, and the three women from Tampa. Gibby strode up and down behind his mahogany desk, medals glinting in the sun-filled room, his ribbons a stream of color as he walked.

"I remember my high-school football coach." General Gibbs's fists punched the air as if he were talking about boxing, not football. "If I'd be in the locker room at the half and I'd say, 'Coach, that other team, they're just too good for us,' he'd say, 'Gibby, you just get a hold of that ball and go, and don't worry if they're good, bad, or indifferent. You just get a hold of that ball and *go!*' Willy?" A shiny-shoed young captain who had been standing by the door leaped to the general's side. "Can't you spook out that coffee we sent for? I'm about falling asleep on my feet here." The captain hurried out.

General Gibbs gripped the arms of his brown leather chair, sat himself down in it and swiveled backward, hands locked behind his head. He allowed himself the luxury of a stretch; then, snapping forward again, turned to the women who were watching his every gesture. "You know," he said, his tone now low and confidential, "I haven't been home in two weeks. Over two weeks. Mrs. Gibbs says she hasn't seen me in so long she knows what you MIA wives must feel like!" He chuckled. Sharon and Fay Clausen smiled; Sandy, Mrs. Doyle, and Jane couldn't quite manage it.

"I'm out there twenty-four hours a day for our POWs and our MIAs, and believe you me, I'm not complaining. I'd stay away from home a year if it would get our boys out of those cages and back where they belong!" He pounded his fist on the desk at this last remark, as if where they belonged were precisely there, in General Fletcher Gibbs's office.

"Excuse me, General Gibbs." Sharon Dornbeck leaned forward, flashing him a full-strength smile. "What I'm afraid of is that they won't see us at all. Alison Fremont went all by herself last month, and she couldn't even get past the guard at the compound gate. To go all that way . . ." Her voice trailed off helplessly.

"Those dirty SOBs!" Gibby was speaking now at battle pitch. "Pardon my French, but I have never seen a group of people who are such savages, and that includes the

Germans, the Japs, and the North Koreans combined!"
Fay Clausen was nodding emphatically. Sandy looked out
the window at Washington's almost leafless trees; she tried
never to think about what the North Vietnamese might
have done to Roy if they found him. "They sign the
Geneva Convention," General Gibbs was continuing, "and
then they turn around and refuse to abide by it. Now how
can you play fair with people like that?"

"You think we'll run into the peace groups over there?"
Fay Clausen was speaking. If there was one thing she
hated, it was the peace groups.

"Hell, no." Gibby smiled, sensing a kinship of views.
"They're hanging around Hanoi these days—which is
where they belong." Laughter all around.

"And remember," Gibby sat forward in his chair, eye-
balling the women for greater intensity, "when you get in
there, don't be afraid to show them pictures of your kids.
God Almighty, some of 'em must have kids." He turned
now to Sharon and flashed her a warm grin. "Remember,
you got a secret weapon. If anything is gonna melt those
stone hearts, it's you little girls."

General Gibbs stood up. Everyone smiled, and the five
women filed out of his office into the labyrinthine cor-
ridors of the Pentagon.

At Dulles Airport, they stood in front of TWA's Flight
642, the wind whistling through their hair, microphones
thrust in front of their faces.

"One of us is Navy, three are Air Force, and one
Army," Sharon answered a reporter's question. "We're
very democratic about it all." She smiled engagingly, and
the cameras clicked.

"Has the State Department set up the appointment for
you with the North Vietnamese delegation in Paris?" a
reporter asked her. "Have they briefed you, given you any
guidelines?"

"No, sir." Sharon's face was sober and sincere. "We've
had no contact whatsoever with the State Department, the
Pentagon, or anyone else. We're going over strictly on our

own to ask the North Vietnamese are we still wives or are we widows."

"Would you just turn a little to face the other ladies, Mrs. Dornbeck? There, that's it." Sharon smiled. More pictures, and the women turned and boarded the gleaming 707, which featured on that evening's flight to Paris, as the stewardess proudly announced, "the movie M*A*S*H*, a comedy presenting a wildly funny picture of war."

8

Letter from the Department of State to an Air Force Wife

Dear Mrs. N. ———————,

I have your letter of Oct. 31, 1967, concerning your desire to travel to North Viet-Nam to visit your husband, Sgt. N.N., USAF, who has been held prisoner in North Viet-Nam since November 1965.

We in the Department, who work constantly on prisoner matters, fully understand your desire to undertake any mission that might help those imprisoned, but in good conscience we are not able to encourage you in an attempt to travel to North Viet-Nam at this time. It is our judgment, after very careful consideration, that such a trip would not help, and could even result in subjecting those imprisoned to further pressures.

In deciding to go to Paris, Sandy knew that other POW/MIA relatives before her had traveled all over the world seeking information about their men. One woman had gone to Vientiane, Laos, to talk directly to the Pathet

Lao. Another saw officials in Moscow. Still others traveled to Geneva, headquarters of the International Red Cross; to Rome to seek the Pope's help; to New Delhi in hopes that the neutral Indians might be able to intercede with the North Vietnamese.

Although these scattered efforts had produced no results, Sandy felt her trip to Paris in the fall of 1969 might be more fruitful. The Paris Peace Talks had started, bringing the North Vietnamese out from behind the Bamboo Curtain to a readily accessible Western capital and, she hoped, changing the political climate. Furthermore, she and the other women felt increasing concern after listening to interviews given by a recently released Naval officer. Lieutenant Robert Frishman had reported conditions of brutality in North Vietnamese prisons, wounds left unattended, and psychological tortures worked on the men. There was now a sharper reason for the women's uneasiness, and a clearly defined place from which to seek information.

The six days they were in Paris, Sandy, Jane, Sharon, Mrs. Doyle and Fay Clausen never once visited the Eiffel Tower. The last day, their taxi driver made a slight detour on his way to the airport and they all craned their necks, but by then they were hardly in a mood for sight-seeing.

They stayed in a small hotel on the Left Bank, run by Madame Guilcourt, a dried-out lady of about fifty, who wore the same black skirt and white silk blouse, shiny from too much ironing, for the entire six days. Her hennaed hair was set in hot-dog rolls, swept up from her ears, and she looked to Sandy like a relic of some G. I. Joe movie. *"Eh bien,"* she would say at every meal, *"vous êtes seulement quatre?"* Clearly she was curious as to why one of them always remained upstairs, but she was too French to ask. When they had finished their *cafés filtres* (Fay and Mrs. Doyle always asked for American coffee, see voo play), the four of them would crowd into the open grillwork elevator and creak their way up to their rooms, take up positions around the phone, and the one member of their group who had not yet eaten would go down for a meal. In this way, none of them ever saw

Paris, but all of them knew they could not possibly miss the call from the North Vietnamese delegation if and when it came. The North Vietnamese had been contacted by a member of the Red Cross, whose name had been given to the women by General Gibbs. Now it was a matter of waiting to hear if an appointment would be granted.

The tedium of being together grated on the women's nerves. Mrs. Doyle was particularly annoying. The mother of an eighteen-year-old boy who had had to secure his mother's consent before enlisting in the Army, she now cried at the slightest provocation. "How could I tell him not to go?" she once asked Fay Clausen, the tears brimming in her eyes. "He always loved guns—from the time he was just a little boy he would play with toy guns, BB guns—you know, pretended he was in the Marines and things. I once got him that big illustrated history of the Second World War—it cost seventeen dollars—from American Heritage, and he read it over and over again." The tears spilled over and down her puffy cheeks. She looked up at Fay Clausen. "Should I have told him not to go?"

Fay said nothing. She felt in no position to give advice. The eldest of her five sons, whose walls were decorated with psychedelic PEACE posters, had angrily confronted her before she left for Paris. "What are you complaining about?" he asked her defiantly. "Dad knew what he was getting into when he joined the Navy. Why should he expect sympathy now?"

Sandy and Jane York shared a large double room. Its two floor-length windows, edged by maroon cut-velvet draperies, opened onto a small balcony overlooking a florist, two antique book stores, and an unshaven, bulbous-nosed man in white cap and apron selling oysters from a cart. During the day all the women would gather in this room with a supply of books, magazines, and cards and wait for the phone to ring. By the fourth day, they had little left to say to each other.

Sharon stood by the window, staring through the glass at a young couple who had stopped at the oyster stand, their arms wound around each other's waists, their breath smoky in the chill November air. She watched the boy buy the girl a plateful of oysters. The girl sucked one oyster from its shell, said something to the boy, they laughed and walked on. "I can't believe that a guy who is six foot one and weighs one hundred eighty pounds just vanished in a puff of smoke." Sharon spoke more to herself than anyone else. "He was third in his class at the Air Force Academy, he was first in survival school. He was such a fantastic pilot. Daddy had them look up his E.R. and he was tops in everything. I *know* he's alive!"

Sandy felt a flash of jealousy at Sharon's clear memories of her husband, and at her faith. "Ring, damn you!" She threw her French fashion magazine on the floor and made hexing signs at the crook-jawed French receiver.

"I'll stay here six months if I have to." Mrs. Doyle looked up from her game of solitaire and began weeping again. "I'm sorry," she apologized, continuing both the game and her tears.

Fay Clausen, who had been sitting quietly in a corner, her fingers pressed to her temples, stood up. "I'm going in the other room. I feel like I'm in communication with Hal, and I want him to tell me what to say to the North Vietnamese." Nobody commented. The others did not think Fay was crazy for believing she could reach her husband by extrasensory perception, only lucky.

Sharon sat down at the slim-legged desk, opened her wallet and began spreading out the pictures she carried of her son and husband. She arranged them first one way, then another. "Did I tell you what Ricky said?" she asked no one in particular. "He said, 'Mommy, let's get a gun and go shoot the bad men who are keepin' Daddy from us.' "

"Yeah, you told us." Jane York looked at Sharon strangely and continued filing her nails. "There," she said. "I think I'll file these into points and pounce on the slanty-eyed bastards!" She made her fingers into claws in the air and sprang toward Sandy. Mrs. Doyle finished her game of solitaire, stretched out her girdled body on a Madame Récamier-like couch and went to sleep.

"Hey, San, let's play casino!" Jane York began dealing

out the cards. Sharon was still seated with her back to the other women. "You know, Sharon," Jane said as she picked up her hand, "you've really got it licked, living with your parents, not a care in the world. Wish I had a setup like that for my kids!" Sharon gave no sign of having heard; she continued rearranging her pictures.

Sandy decided to build eights. "You ever think of moving in with your folks or Earl's?" she asked Jane, who looked up, surprised at Sandy's naïveté.

"Girl, you know what my father said? He said Earl got just what he deserved for messing with The Man in the first place! Oh, ho, ho, ho!" Jane reached over and swooped up the cards. "Big casino!"

Later she glanced up from her hand. "Hey, San, I changed it. I'm not gonna wear the white pants suit when Earl comes home." She looked off toward the streets of Paris, indulging in the MIA wives' favorite fantasy. "I'm gonna wear this real tight one-piece purple jump suit."

"Oh, yeah?" Sandy made her voice low and gravelly. "Well, you know what I'm gonna wear when Roy comes walking through that door? Nothing!"

She and Jane exploded with laughter. Mrs. Doyle awakened with a start and looked over at them questioningly. "Go back to sleep, Mrs. Doyle," Sandy soothed her. Mrs. Doyle obediently lowered her head, and Sandy and Jane giggled. Sharon gave the two girls a look of disgust and went back to rearranging her pictures. The door opened and Fay Clausen wandered back in. "It won't work," she stated. "I'm too nervous. It only works when I feel very serene and calm."

They were deciding whose turn it was to stay upstairs during dinner when the silent black French phone suddenly rang.

The North Vietnamese compound was located in a suburb of Paris called Choisy-le-Roi. The building was made of slate-gray stone and set well back from the road, with a driveway leading up to the front gate. It was unpretentious as official residences in France go, but nevertheless looked part of the heritage of Louis XIV,

Napoleon, and De Gaulle except for two small details: the red and yellow North Vietnamese flag fluttering from its turret, and the volleyball court visible through its spiked iron fence. Inside, it was furnished with modern bamboo chairs and low teak tables. The desk and chair used by Mr. Than, one of the chief North Vietnamese delegates, were Louis XV; on the wall behind him was a large portrait of Ho Chi Minh. To one side of Mr. Than sat a male stenographer, expressionless, his pen poised. In one corner of the room a North Vietnamese man stood silently watching everything, never speaking yet somehow seeming to be in charge of the proceedings.

The women sat in a semi-circle around Mr. Than's desk, each balancing a blue-and-white scroll-patterned teacup in one hand and pictures of their sons and husbands in the other. No one drank the tea.

Mr. Than nodded his head slightly to Jane York. She put the teacup down on the table. "This is my husband Earl Arthur York," she began, her voice soft and nervous, "Captain in the United States Air Force. This picture was taken five years ago."

"We will not need information on when the picture was taken," Mr. Than interrupted her.

"Oh, I'm sorry. He went down over Minh, May 30, 1967." She held out the picture of her husband, which Mr. Than put to one side of his desk without a glance.

"Roy Dean Lawton, Air Force Lieutenant." Sandy felt her heart pounding. There was no noise in the room except the scratching of the stenographer's pen. "He was shot down October 14, 1967, over Hon Gai." She surrendered the picture. "I've had no word since that date."

"This is my son, John Joseph Doyle." Mrs. Doyle handed Mr. Than not one but three photographs. "He's just a corporal in the Army but he was on the Medevacs—You know, the rescue helicopters?" No reaction from Mr. Than. "February 2, 1967. He . . . he . . . only nineteen years old . . ."

"Harold Jens Clausen," Fay cut in before Mrs. Doyle could begin weeping, "Commander, United States Navy. The information I was given was that he went down February 22, 1966, over Minh." She paused and lowered her voice. "However, I have reason to believe it was closer to Hanoi. Please," she turned to the stenographer, "could you put down 'Minh or somewhere closer to Hanoi?' " Fay unfolded an accordion of photos and clumsily tried to show them to the silent man in the corner as well as to Mr. Than. "These are our five sons. Please, it would mean everything to them if I could just tell them their father is still alive. He's been missing for more than three years."

"Yes, you have already mentioned the duration of Commander Clausen's absence. We have noted it." There was the barest suggestion of a smile on Mr. Than's face. The stenographer scratched on. The silent man in the corner remained silent.

"Richard Whittier Dornbeck, Captain, United States Air Force . . ." As Sharon spoke, a leathery-faced Vietnamese servant woman, dressed in white tunic and black pants, slipped into the room, bearing a red lacquered tray filled with small white-dusted squares. Each of the women took one, politely murmuring their gratitude. Sharon had finished speaking. There was a pause, as the women looked at Mr. Than expectantly. He smiled graciously at them. "You would perhaps like more tea?"

"Oh, no. Thank you." The pause lengthened. Jane bit into the white square, which looked exactly like bean curd covered with dust. "This is delicious—is it a kind of cake?" she smiled up at Mr. Than.

He smiled back. "No, it's candy. You like it?"

"I sure do. It's delicious."

Mrs. Doyle took a rabbit-like nibble of hers. "Not too sweet. I don't like candy too sweet. I mean, it's sweet, but it's not *too* sweet." She smiled nervously at Mr. Than, trying to shove the piece of cardboard-tasting candy into one cheek.

"I would like to read you something." Mr. Than held out his hand and the stenographer passed him a sheet of thin rice paper. Teacups and candy were forgotten as the women strained forward to listen intently. Perhaps he would reveal a list of captured men.

"This is from Madame Trong." Mr. Than looked up at them coolly. "A letter written to you on behalf of the women of the Democratic Republic of Vietnam. 'Dear Wives of American Soldiers,'" he began, "'why do you weep and wail? Why do you come begging for information? Your children are safe. Our children are maimed by your husbands' bombs. You wish to know what to tell your children? Tell your children their fathers are murderers of North Vietnamese children. . . .'" Suddenly the incongruity of the scene struck Sandy: this little Oriental man, surrounded by bamboo furniture and the crystal trappings of royalist France, was reading her a moral lecture, and she realized she would do anything not to offend him, anything to find out *something* from him.

He finished his letter and eyed them levelly. Sharon spoke. "Mr. Than, we aren't political. We're just wives and mothers. We aren't rich people, but we will do anything you say if only you will give us some word about our men. We can raise money for a hospital in your country, a school, anything you want. . . ."

"There is one thing you can do." Mr. Than looked not at Sharon but at all of them. They leaned forward eagerly. "Join the others in your country who urge your government to end the war."

The women sat quietly in their seats, their faces impassive. Mr. Than stood up. "Would you please come with me into the next room?" They followed him through carved double doors into a smaller room furnished only with rude wooden camp chairs, a 16-millimeter projector and a screen. The silent man slipped in behind them and took up his post at the back of the room. The women seated themselves, and the lights went out.

A Vietnamese girl of about eight, standing in front of the rubble of a house, smiled out at them. Except she could only smile with half her face; the other half looked as if it had been dissolved and melted together again in a new and hideous way. Her nose, what must have been her cheek, and part of her mouth were now only scarred masses of skin, all running together. She waved at the camera grotesquely. Sandy felt as if she were going to be sick. Two boys, perhaps five and eight years old, were poking through the wreckage of a building. One of them held up part of a bomb casing. Stamped on the metal were the words, MADE IN THE USA. The camera was inside a hospital hit by a bomb. Patients lying on the floor, beds overturned, an old man wandering toward the camera, dazed from shock. He turned toward the camera; there was no skin on his upper arm. Sharon pressed her handkerchief to her mouth. Jane looked at a spot just above the screen. The children's ward of the hospital. An emaciated boy of about ten waited to see the doctor, seated because he had no legs. Two mothers rocked their blood-covered babies. Though the film was silent, Sharon felt she could hear the infants' screams. One mother turned to the camera, and Sharon felt the look in the woman's eyes almost as a physical pain. "Please," she whispered, "just turn it off!" Fay grabbed Sharon's arm, pressing her to be quiet.

The lights went on. No one looked at anyone else. The women filed silently out of the room. Mr. Than escorted them down the moiré-walled halls to the door of the building. He shook each of their hands and assured them with a pleasant smile that he would let them know if he had any word of their husbands.

In the taxi back to the hotel, there were long stretches of silence. The air was damp and cold, and they kept the windows tightly shut. The landmarks of Paris flashed by them unnoticed.

"How could they show us that film?" Jane was snapping and unsnapping her purse. "Those babies . . ."

"They're barbarians, that's what they are." Mrs. Doyle began weeping, and for once no one tried to stop her.

Sharon pulled out her picture of Ricky and concentrated on trying to straighten out the edges, which were bent from being in her wallet. "You okay?" Sandy asked her.

"You know what Ricky said?" Sharon never took her eyes off the picture. "He said, 'Mommy, let's get a gun and go shoot the bad men who are keepin' Daddy from us.'" Sandy looked at her sharply.

Fay, seated in the front of the taxi, turned back to face the others. "Listen, it was horrible," she said, "but the thing to remember is that this was a propaganda film." Mrs. Doyle nodded, dabbing at her eyes.

Sandy looked blindly through the taxi windows at the streets of Paris. She had spent a good part of her savings and considerable hope to come to Paris, only to find exactly nothing. Paris provided her with no answers. Only questions. In her mind she was seeing the eight-year-old girl with only half a smile. Never, since she had met Roy, and in all the time he was missing, had she allowed herself to think, to visualize in human terms, what it was that Roy *did* in Vietnam. "You know something?" she said softly, still staring out the window. "They think *we're* the barbarians."

9

Letter from the Department of the Air Force

Dear Air Force Next of Kin,

In the last newsletter, we advised you of the 1 July 1969 conversion to the Social Security Account Number as the Military Service Number. By way of further explanation, an officer's service number is now expressed 123–45–6789 FR (Regular officer), 123–45–6789 FV (Reserve officer), or 123–45–6789 FG (Air National Guard officer). The service number for an enlisted member is written with a prefix, i.e., FR 123–45–6789.

We have been advised by the State Department that when attempting to forward mail to the missing or captured member, you should use the service number used by the member at the time he was lost from military control regardless of the changeover on 1 July. This is the number he will have provided to his captors, and he may not be aware of the changeover.

Indirectly, the abortive Paris trip launched Sharon Dorn-beck on her career as a luncheon circuit public speaker.

When she got back from Paris, her father and Ricky met her at the airport. She rushed into her father's arms. "Oh, Daddy, you were so right! They're savages!" Ricky had wound himself around her leg and she quickly picked him up, hugged him, and got into the car.

"I tried to tell you, Princess," Jerry said on the way home. "It's like gettin' into a pool with a man-eating shark. He's just got to eat you up alive 'cause that's how he's built and that's all he knows."

"It was such a waste." She closed her eyes and put her head back against the seat, trying to wipe out the images of maimed children which kept asserting themselves. "Is Sharon sick?" Ricky turned to his grandfather.

"No, she's just a little tired. Hey, Tiger!" Jerry took one hand off the wheel and punched Ricky playfully in the stomach, "after we put Mommy in bed, you know any little boys want to go down to Ruggle's for an ice-cream soda?"

"Me!" Ricky jumped up and down on the seat.

"Good! Sharon, honey," Jerry spoke across the child, "maybe it wasn't a waste. I'm sorry you put yourself through it. But when you're feelin' better, I want you to get out there and tell people what happened, let 'em know what we're up against. You want to help Dick? That's the way to do it."

Sharon nodded obediently, eyes still closed. The following Friday, at her father's suggestion and at the invitation of the local American Legion post, to which Jerry Gundersen belonged, Sharon was the featured speaker in an appealing, emotionally wrenching presentation of the POW/MIA problem. Included in it was an implied defense of the administration.

For Sandy Lawton, too, the trip to Paris was a watershed. The night after she came home, back to her empty apartment, she sat down and made a phone call.

"Hello?" Alan's voice at the other end of the line was

barely audible, almost overwhelmed by loud orchestral music.

"Alan? It's Sandy Lawton," she shouted.

"Just a minute, I have to turn this thing down." There was a loud blast of trumpets, a clash of cymbals, and then a soft flurry of violins. "Hello, Sandy Lawton." Alan's voice sounded surprised and, she thought, pleased. "Where have you been keeping yourself? I haven't seen you in the library."

"Oh, I had to go out of town for a little while." She was doodling penciled figure eights on a small white pad as she sat barefoot on an unpainted wooden chair, her toes curled around the rung.

"Oh? How come? Everything okay?"

"Well, I . . ."

"I know, you don't want to talk about it."

"No, I don't."

There was an uncomfortable pause, and then Alan asked, "Is there something you *do* want to talk about? You did call me, didn't you?"

Sandy shifted in the hard chair. She had called him on an impulse, not even quite sure herself what she would say. She only knew that she had felt physically incapable of opening a book, the unadorned white walls of her apartment suddenly seeming like a cell to her. She supposed she had called him out of an overwhelming desire to *do* something, to control the course of her own life in some small way. "I just . . . Remember, you told me to read the book by Piaget?" Sandy heard herself saying.

"Oh, yeah."

"Well, I have quite a few questions, and I thought we could get together sometime and discuss it maybe." She felt the perspiration between her breasts as she waited for Alan to say something.

"Give me your address, and I'll pick you up in twenty minutes." She smiled, and, as she gave him her address, wondered in panic what she would wear.

The atmosphere inside El Club Linda Vista was close and murky. Pinpoints of red and yellow light played through the smoky air, casting a ruddy glow on the faces of people sipping tequila cocktails or smearing guacamole on their tortillas. Behind the bar, a man in shiny black-pleated pants and white blouse with triple-pouffed red-and-white sleeves was rhythmically gyrating a silver cocktail shaker in time to "Piel Canela" on the jukebox.

Sandy carefully scooped up a spoonful of red-and-green relish, as she had seen Alan do, smeared it on top of her beef taco and bit in. Her nostrils flared, her mouth was aflame, tears poured out of her eyes. She dropped the taco, fanned her mouth with one hand, and grabbed for water with the other. Alan was laughing at her. "Who told you to put so much on?"

"You could have at least told me it was hot!" she gasped, laughing and wiping her eyes with the napkin.

"You want a beer?" She nodded. *"¡Oiga!"* He called to the waiter. *"¡Dos cervezas, por favor!"*

Sandy put her napkin in her lap, checking to see that none of her eye make-up had come off on it. "I didn't know you could speak Spanish."

"Oh"—he shrugged—"I don't speak it very well." He leaned out of the red vinyl banquette, craning his neck toward the departing waiter. *"Tráigalos ahora,"* he called, *"la señorita la quiere ahorita."*

"Alan, you're great!" Sandy looked at him respectfully. "I studied it for two years in high school and never got past '*Me llamo* Sandy Fraser.'"

He smiled across at her. "Hey, how could you live in Florida all this time and not have tried a Latin restaurant?"

"I haven't even seen the men who wrestle with the alligators, and that's supposed to be the big deal around here."

"Neither have I. Let's go together sometime. Want to?"

Sandy nodded and busily fixed herself another taco, this time with just a dab of hot sauce.

"You know what else I'd like to do?" Alan was chewing his taco with great satisfaction. A speck of green relish had gotten caught in the reddish hairs of his beard, and she resisted the impulse to lean over and pick it off. "I'd like to drive down to the Keys— Papa's old turf."

"Your father?"

"No." He swallowed the taco. "Ernest Hemingway, his nickname was 'Papa.' " Sandy nodded, embarrassed by her ignorance. *"My* father is a CPA in Brooklyn." Alan grinned. A nasal baritone began moaning *"Te amo, corazón,"* lingering with full vibrato on the *-zón.*

"You come from Brooklyn?" Sandy's voice was incredulous. "I never met anybody from Brooklyn."

"Yeah, well, I guess out in North Platte, Nebraska, you wouldn't. Jesus, North Platte, Nebraska!" Alan pronounced it as if it were some spot on the other side of the moon. "I bet you were a high-school cheerleader, and your boy friend was the football captain."

"Unh-uh." Sandy sipped the beer which had arrived, and looked at him teasingly.

"No?"

"He was on the basketball team." She giggled. Alan laughed and leaned forward, his elbows on the white tablecloth. She noticed the dark hair on his arms and at the throat of his blue-and-white striped sport shirt. "Hey," he said, "tell me one of your cheers."

"Here? Are you crazy?"

"Sure, come on!"

"No!"

"Why not?"

"Because!"

"Just say the words."

Sandy sighed and shrugged her shoulders. "Oh, all right." She glanced around to make sure no one was listening, folded her arms across each other on the table and bent forward toward him. "Acka-lacka ching . . . Oh, Alan, I feel like an idiot." She covered her face with her hands.

"Nobody's listening— Come on!" He pulled her hands down.

"All right." She folded her arms again. "But I can't look at you when I say it." She focused her attention on the stein of beer, its head tinted orange in the red and yellow Linda Vista light. "Acka-lacka ching, acka-lacka chow. Acka-lacka ching ching, chow, chow, chow. Booma-lacka booma-lacka, sis boom bah. North Platte, North Platte, rah rah rah!"

"Terrific!" Alan was applauding. "Tell me again, acka-what?"

In the nearly deserted parking lot in front of the restaurant, Alan stood in front of his car, elbows bent out at his sides, knees spread apart, a bearded cheerleader facing Sandy in the imaginary stands. "Acka-lacka CHING! Acka-lacka CHOW! Acka-lacka ching ching, CHOW CHOW CHOW!" His arms moved forward, and the red neon sign of El Club Linda Vista blinked in rhythm to the cheer. "Booma-lacka, booma-lacka, sis boom bah. North Platte, North Platte, RAH RAH RAH!" His voice boomed out on the last line, and Sandy dissolved in laughter.

"On the last 'rah' you're supposed to jump up in the air," she told him. "Like this. NORTH PLATTE, NORTH PLATTE, RAH RAH RAH!" She leaped up into the air, flinging her arms back so that they almost touched her legs, her blue jersey miniskirt billowing out like a parachute, and gracefully landed again on the asphalt of the parking lot. "Hooray for North Platte!" Alan applauded, and they both laughed.

"Why do you like it so much?" she asked him.

"It's like folk poetry," Alan told her earnestly, while opening the car door for her.

"*Poetry!*" She got in the car. "I mean it rhymes, but I wouldn't call it poetry."

Alan walked around, got in his side and started up his Volkswagen. "I really think somebody should collect all those cheers and make them into a book."

Sandy giggled. "Who'd buy it besides you?"

They drove through the narrow, crowded streets of downtown Tampa and Alan headed out toward the highway along the beach. There was a full moon in the sky, and shining through the Volkswagen window, it outlined in silvery profile the fuzz of Alan's hair, his spectacles, the harsh straight slope of his nose, and the surprisingly soft mass of his beard. Sandy's pocketbook was on the seat between them. She sat close to the door on her side of the car, not looking at him.

"You go back home at all?" he asked.

"When Janis, that's my kid sister, when she had her first baby. Now she's got two."

"God, how old is she?"

"Twenty."

"Fast worker." Alan turned right off the highway toward Sandy's block of modern brick apartments.

"Yeah, well, there's not much to do in North Platte. Everybody goes to bed early." She giggled, and Alan laughed. He pulled up in front of her building. "Hey," he turned to her, "you have a good time tonight?"

"Alan, it was the most fun I've had since . . . well, you know." She picked up her pocketbook with one hand, clutching the car door with the other. "That's why I hardly ever go home. Everybody sits around and talks about my 'situation.' My mother's always coming out with things like, 'Well, this is the hand God dealt you, you'll have to live with it.' "

"Yichh!" Alan laughed.

"Yichh is right!"

They got out of the car and walked through the heavy glass doors of Sandy's building into the carpeted lobby. She noticed how lankily he moved. "Hey," he said as the elevator stopped at four, "we never got to Piaget."

"What? Oh." She stood in the elevator, embarrassed. The automatic door was about to close again, and they both reached out at the same time to keep it open.

"After you," he laughed, and she ducked under his arm. He walked down the corridor next to her, hands in the pockets of his navy slacks, not looking at her. "I'm *glad* you called me. . . . I was thinking about calling you the other day, but I wasn't really sure you'd speak to me."

At the door to her apartment, Sandy pulled out her key chain, a tiny, translucent blue mermaid, liquid sloshing inside its curvy body, keys hanging from its tail. Sandy held on to it and turned expectantly to Alan. "I really had

a good time." Alan was staring down at the carpet, silent.
"Thanks," she said.

He looked at her. "Maybe I'll see you in the library tomorrow."

"Yeah, I'll be there in the afternoon." Still he did not
move. She could feel the space between them.

"This is the way you want it, isn't it, Mrs. Lawton?"
He looked directly into her eyes. "G'night." He quickly
reached over, chucked her gently under the chin, and
walked down the acanthus-patterned carpet toward the
elevator.

She let herself into her apartment, her hands shaking.
Whether from relief or disappointment, she was not sure.

10

Editorial in New York Daily News **Reprinted and Mailed by the Department of the Air Force to All Next of Kin.**

A Voice of Courage

"I would never demonstrate against my government. That would dishonor my husband."

A courageous woman spoke these words Wednesday night in Paris while numbers of her countrymen were bending every effort to egg the U.S. into a quick pull-out and sell-out in Vietnam.

The woman was Mrs. R. J. Her husband, Cmdr. C. J., has been a prisoner in North Vietnam since March 1968.

Mrs. J. had gone to Paris to ask North Vietnamese delegates to intercede for release of sick and wounded prisoners on humanitarian grounds.

Their answer was as crude as it was cruel: wives of American captives can speed the release of their mates only if they join in

demonstrations to pressure the U.S. into a
surrender in Vietnam.

It would seem [our domestic dissenters] are
less finicky than Mrs. J. when it comes to
matters of honor.

Among the protesters, however, must be
many still not blind to their country's interest. For them, we pass along a suggestion
made by Herbert Klein, director of com-
munications for President Richard M. Nixon:

Our hope is that the next time they demonstrate they would do so in a way that would
help us—for example, demonstrating to
bring the prisoners home from North
Vietnam.

Room 2218 of the Rayburn Building in Washington,
D. C., was just large enough to accommodate the crowd
which assembled on a cold, bloodless December morning
for the House Armed Services Committee hearing on the
POW/MIA problem. Although only fifteen of the forty-
one congressmen on the Committee were present, the
room was thronged with assorted next of kin, casualty
officers, representatives from the State Department, Pentagon, Red Cross, and press.

Mary Kaye Buell was sitting at the witness table, patiently awaiting her turn to testify. To her, the hearing
resembled a gigantic tennis match whose players were
aiming not to win but only to keep the ball arcing smoothly back and forth across the net, always within the safety
of the base lines. No surprises. No tricks. Just a steady
flow of predictable plays, by the end of which the congressmen could go on to other business, satisfied that they
had listened, and the next of kin could go back home to
Texas and Florida and Colorado, satisfied that they had
been heard.

Mary Kaye listened to Sharon Dornbeck, immaculate in her white wool princess-style dress, reading aloud from carefully prepared notes.

"In summary, Mr. Chairman, the trip to Paris which I have just described could no doubt be considered a failure, since none of us has heard from the North Vietnamese delegation as to the status of our men. We went to Paris asking if we were wives or widows. We still don't know the answer. When I got off the plane, my father had brought my son to the airport to meet me, and my little boy said, 'Mommy, did the man tell you? Is Daddy there?' I had to say, 'Ricky, I don't know.' " Here Sharon's voice faltered. She quickly reached for her monogrammed handkerchief, and patted the moisture from her palms. Some of the congressmen behind the long table facing the wives and the rest of the audience looked down at their papers and manila folders, moved yet embarrassed.

"And yet"— Sharon's voice was firmer now, the congressmen looked up, relieved— "I have told my son that there is one thing I do know. I am secure in the knowledge that the United States government will do everything in its power to obtain the release of our men and to bring them back safely to their wives and parents and children. It is truly an honor for me to appear before you today. On behalf of the next of kin of many men missing and imprisoned in Southeast Asia, I thank you." Sharon's face relaxed into a sweet but tentative smile. The Chairman, a white-haired man whose Southern accent was even more pronounced than Sharon's, cleared his throat.

"Miz' Dornbeck, I think I can safely say we have never witnessed greater fortitude and courage in the witness chair than that exemplified by you brave girls." The room rang with applause.

Maybe she's right, Mary Kaye thought. Why make a scene? What good will it do? She reached into her pocketbook for a package of Life Savers and popped one in her mouth.

"Will all the next of kin in the audience please stand up?" Feeling like a prize exhibit at a farm show, Mary Kaye got to her feet and stood through a round of applause. You either play it their way like Sharon or you don't go to the game, she thought.

More words were lobbed back and forth. "The plight of our loved ones." "Savage and inhumane treatment." "We will not abandon our brave men." A message from President Nixon was read. A message from Secretary Laird. A Pentagon official stated that there were next of kin in every single state of the union including Hawaii. A congressman expressed his conviction that a stepped-up bombing campaign would let the enemy know we mean business. The hell with it, thought Mary Kaye, it's not worth it. She examined her fingernails and decided to blow a few bucks on a manicure as soon as the meeting was over. Then she'd go shopping, pick up some souvenirs for the kids. A sports encyclopedia for Pete. He'd read *that,* at least. And a model of the Washington Monument for the girls, one encased in a glass ball which snowed when you turned it over. What could she get for Joe? she wondered. Her thoughts were interrupted by the booming statement of Congressman Conners.

"I am sitting here just wondering if we haven't overlooked a mighty strong weapon in our efforts to get our prisoners released." Conners had dark straight hair framing a face that looked well tanned, by sun when possible, by sun lamp when necessary, Mary Kaye thought. He waved his pencil as if to punctuate his points. "That weapon is a prayer." Mary Kaye blinked. Prayer! "Never underestimate its power, my friends. I am therefore recommending to the President that we set aside a special day, a day of prayer for our missing and captured in Vietnam." His words fell on Mary Kaye like pebbles in an empty pail. Prayer!

She thought back to earlier that morning, when she and Margaret Holroyd had gone to mass at St. Matthew's on their way to the House hearing. Margaret had paused before entering the church. "Mary Kaye," she asked carefully, "who do you pray for in there?"

"The kids," Mary Kaye answered, "that they'll turn out all right, that they'll be normal. I guess you pray for John."

Margaret had shaken her head. "I pray for myself, that I'll be able to get through it without losing my mind." She had looked questioningly at Mary Kaye, as though wondering if such a selfish request of the Lord was appropriate.

"Good a prayer as any," Mary Kaye replied easily, as they stepped inside the church.

Congressman Conners was sitting back now, receiving tribute from the assembled multitude for his suggestion of a day of prayer. Mary Kaye folded her arms, not even pretending to join in the applause. Her resolve, lulled by the predictability of the previous exchanges, had been rudely smacked to life again by Congressman Conners. Prayer, eh?

She was the last of the wives to speak. By now it was lunchtime, and certain congressmen were surreptitiously looking at their watches. Pentagon people were slipping papers into their brief cases. The man from the State Department was wondering if he could slip out without anybody noticing.

Mary Kaye spoke without notes, her voice adopting the exaggerated, lilting cadence she usually reserved for her skirmishes with the military. "My husband has been a prisoner for four and one-half years," she began firmly. "During that time public opinion has been mightily aroused. Diplomatic efforts have been made. Resolutions have been passed in both House and Senate. And, may I assure you in particular, Congressman Conners, more prayers have been said by more lonely families than you could ever know." Conners' eyes looked pale and hard behind his horn-rimmed glasses. "May I tell you therefore, I am sick and tired of words, be they addressed to the Good Lord or anybody else." She looked at the fourteen congressmen flanking their chairman, loyal but gullible disciples. At the far end was Congressman Bradley, a tiny, bald man, who had once tried to introduce legislation which would bring the war to a halt. He nodded at Mary Kaye, as though to say, go on, don't stop now.

Mary Kaye swallowed and continued. "If we want our men back, we must face up to the fact that this war is not merely immoral and illegal; it is simply a mistake. My husband is wasting his life. So are other prisoners. *And it is for nothing!*" She paused and looked around the silent room. "Gentlemen," she continued, "the course of action we should take seems very clear to me, and it has nothing to do with prayer. If we want to get our men back, we must set a withdrawal date. Unless that is done, I don't believe my four children will ever see their father again. Thank you."

No one applauded.

Finally Congressman Bradley spoke. "Mrs. Buell, I am over here at the end, not because I am being ostracized but because we are seated by seniority." He smiled like a mischievous toddler, and the room resounded with laughter. "You can run for Chairman any time you want to, Mr. Bradley," the Chairman drawled. "Thank you, I just might do that," Bradley replied. "But, as I was saying to Mrs. Buell, I am new to this, having been involved for the last year only."

"How fortunate for you, sir," Mary Kaye threw in. "My children and I have been involved for the last four and one-half years." Then she bit her lip. Why was she picking on her one ally?

Bradley seemed oblivious. "Have you any impression of how your husband is being treated?"

Mary Kaye folded her arms and leaned her elbows on the table. "If you have seen the letters from the prisoners, you will know that they are permitted to write almost nothing about their treatment or anything else. Lieutenant Frishman, when he was released recently, had lost forty-five pounds; Seaman Hegdahl, sixty-five pounds. Other releasees describe malnutrition, malaria and other diseases, wounds unattended for years at a time, isolation from each other. All I know for sure is that my husband can still hold a pencil in his hand and write a few lines every six months.

"Brian was thirty-two when he was captured. He is now almost thirty-seven. Most men in their thirties are advancing in their careers and raising their families. My husband has wasted these years in a prison camp for what I have come to believe is a totally unworthy cause." Sharon Dornbeck, seated next to Mary Kaye turned her head away.

Congressman Bradley wanted Mary Kaye to press on. He fed her another cue. "My own views on the war are well known; I would have to agree with you." I don't think two of us are quite enough, Mary Kaye thought. But it's nice to have a friend in a strange land. "Would you say Captain Buell shares these views?"

"I cannot answer that, sir. I haven't spoken to him recently." I've gone this far, she thought, I might as well pull out all the stops. "I think, however, were he to be deposited on my doorstep tomorrow, he would discover that far from suffering from this war, most of his fellow Americans have occupied themselves with the purchase of their second or *third* car, their second or *third* color-television set."

Congressman Conners leaned over toward the Chairman, his hand shielding his mouth, and whispered, "I wish we could get Captain Buell out of that prison camp and put his wife in instead."

When the meeting broke up, Mary Kaye walked toward Congressman Bradley, intending somehow to express her gratitude to the little man. But he disappeared into the crowd and she found herself standing alone, looking at the congressmen clustered around Sharon, feeling like a wallflower at a teen dance, all dressed up and nobody to talk to. Margaret, her brown hair in little tendrils around her face, edged her way through the wives and mothers and placed herself staunchly at Mary Kaye's side.

"Well, Mary Kaye," she grinned, "there goes your invitation to the White House to the President's tea."

Mary Kaye felt a surge of affection for Margaret who she knew disagreed with everything Mary Kaye had said, including the fact that she had said it, and yet placed friendship above ideology. Mary Kaye inclined her head toward Sharon, who was graciously receiving the adulation of the crowd, a queen with her subjects. "Miss Pink-and-White over there will get two this year."

Margaret giggled and putting a protective arm around

Mary Kaye's shoulder, propelled her toward the door. Mary Kaye was suddenly exhilarated. What had she said that was so terrible, after all? Besides, Brian was already in a prison camp. What more could anybody do to her? "Margaret, I have a sudden mad urge to go on a shopping spree." She started to laugh. Just as they reached the door, a thin, slack-breasted wife stopped them. "I hope your husband is satisfied with staying a captain," the woman said, "because after your performance today, he doesn't have much chance of getting beyond it."

Mary Kaye was instantly sober. Without another word, she and Margaret made their way through the long halls of the Rayburn Building and out to the cold rainy streets of Washington.

A few days later, when the Washington trip was forgotten in the realities of teaching the causes of the Civil War to her sixth graders, Mary Kaye asked Phil Goratt, the gym teacher at her school, if he would mind driving her home. A big, solid man, with a ruddy complexion and graying hair, he was the kind of friend she could count on to give her a lift if her car was in the shop or to talk common sense when she was concerned about her children. "What *do* you think is bugging Joe, Phil?" she was asking him. "You know, he was caught stealing money from Jimmy Mason's locker a few weeks ago? Now why would he do a thing like that? He has plenty of money. I see to that."

He smiled at her, and she noticed he was still wearing the whistle around his neck from school. "Mary Kaye, you know your trouble? You worry too much. All kids steal. All kids steal, and almost all kids grow out of stealing. Don't bug him about it."

They turned into her street in suburban Silver Grove, and she watched the kids playing ball scamper out of the way of the car. "It's just that, well, you read so much about the problems of kids in father-absent homes—and with a wretch of a mother like me . . . I don't know, I just don't seem to be able to talk to him any more."

"Want me to try to talk with him and see what I can do?"

"Oh, would you, Phil? That would be great."

They had pulled up in front of the Buells' split-level house. Joe and Pete were playing basketball in the driveway. "Hey, Mr. Goratt," Pete yelled out. "Watch this!" A tricky sideways dribble was executed, followed by a perfect swish.

"Good shot!" Phil called out. Joe had picked up the ball and was dribbling it now. "How about you, Joe?" The dribbling continued. No answer. "Hey," Phil called out, "how would you boys like me to take you to a ball game sometime?"

"Great!" Pete's face broke into a smile. Joe dribbled down one side of the driveway, around the stone marker in the grass, and back up the other side of the drive.

"Joe!" Mary Kaye got out of the car. "Did you hear what Mr. Goratt said?"

"I heard him," Joe muttered, still dribbling the ball.

She walked over to her son. "I don't get it," she said to him softly, so Phil couldn't hear. "I thought you wanted to go to a game."

"Not with him," Joe muttered angrily. Dribbling the ball very fast away from his mother, he arced a perfect basket, retrieved the ball, and went inside.

Puzzled and embarrassed, she turned toward Phil in the waiting car. "Thanks for the lift," she called. "We'll have to let you know about the game. See you in school tomorrow."

He waved back and pulled away, leaving her alone again with the children.

11

News Release from the Defense Department

The following statement was issued today by Secretary of Defense Melvin R. Laird:

"Sunday, November 29, has been declared a National Day of Prayer and Concern for the hundreds of U.S. servicemen who are prisoners of war or missing in action in Southeast Asia.

"I know that the hundreds of wives, children and parents who have sought for so long to learn the status of their loved ones, deeply appreciate the prayers and concern of all Americans on this occasion."

Walton State's brochure tried to give the Boat Pond an aura of romance, claiming that if a boy and girl walked around its circumference three times, they would surely marry. This was perhaps eight-year-old Walton State's only tradition, and Alan Webber suspected it was created by the promotional writers in much the same way the college itself was created, on the spur of the moment, in response to necessity. The reality was far more prosaic. The Boat Pond was so called because, before Walton had sprung up around it, it was reputedly used by children to sail

91

toy boats across. Now, however, it had become mainly a
receptacle for beer cans or an occasional drunken student
fulfilling a fraternity pledge by plunging in.

Sandy was seated on an olive Army blanket, spread out
on the grassy slopes near the pond, examining the long,
almost straight tree branch Alan was holding out to her.

"No."

"How come?" Alan asked.

"It's the wrong thickness, and it doesn't have knobs on
the ends."

"What do you need knobs for?"

"Balance."

"Christ, you're choosy." He stretched out beside her.
"All right, I'll buy you one." He closed his eyes. The sun
shining down on the thick emerald carpet grass cast a
shimmer in the air and glanced off Alan's glasses.

"Okay," she said brightly, all the while yearning to
curl up next to him, "but you're gonna be disappointed,
I'm warning you. I wasn't that good. If my mother'd let
me go to twirling camp, it would have been a different
story."

Alan opened his eyes. "Twirling camp!"

"Sure. All the girls who win trophies have been to twirling camp."

"Twirling camp." Alan smiled to himself and closed
his eyes again.

"Alan, listen to this assignment. 'Bring in three songs
for five-year-olds and three songs for six-year-olds and be
prepared to explain your choices.' Isn't that dumb? Certain
five-year-olds are smarter than certain six-year-olds. At
least you have to find out their backgrounds. The assignment seems so pointless."

"You're catching on fast." Without opening his eyes,
Alan removed his steel-framed spectacles and tucked them
into his shirt pocket.

"You don't think much of Walton, do you?"

"It's hardly the summit of my ambitions to sit around
in this diploma mill preparing a bunch of dumb-bunnies
to be teachers." He opened his eyes and sat up, tipping an
imaginary hat to her. "Present company excepted."

"That's okay. I don't claim to be smart."

"Yeah, but you got potential."

"Honest?"

"Stick with me."

A few days ago, Alan had taken her to a showing of *Citizen Kane* at the campus film society. Afterward, they joined some of Alan's friends for pizza, and Sandy listened in silent admiration as they exchanged occult film lore. "At least the critics are giving Gregg Toland credit for the part he played," one girl had said, twisting her feather necklace.

"What part did he play?" Sandy ventured. "Was he Jed?"

"That was Joseph Cotten," the girl replied patronizingly, "Gregg Toland was the cinematographer." She turned to the boy next to her. "Did you hear that? She thought Toland was *in* the film."

Alan draped his arm along the booth behind Sandy, and in the coolest voice said, "Rochelle, you're a fucking intellectual snob, you know that?"

Sandy smiled as she remembered his comment and closed the psychology book she had been pretending to study. "Hey, Alan? What *is* the summit of your ambition, or however you put it?"

"You really want to know?"

"Of course."

He pulled up a dandelion and began pulling out its petals. "I'd like to run an experimental school, ungraded, no marks or any of that crap, and really find out how kids learn." He threw down the stem, waiting for her reaction.

"That would be fabulous! Why don't you do it?"

"What do you suggest, close my eyes and turn around three times and there it will be?"

"Come on, now, you can do it."

"If I listen to you long enough, I probably will." Alan yawned and stretched out.

Yesterday they had had a terrible argument. She had refused to sign an antiwar petition which was circulating around the college. "Why?" Alan had asked. "You want the war to end, don't you?"

"Yes, but I'm married to someone in the military. It would look terrible!"

Alan was disgusted. *"He's* in the military— *You* aren't. Besides, you don't relinquish your civil rights when you join the military."

"Look," she said, her voice growing querulous, "just because I agree with some of your ideas on the war doesn't mean I have to go around signing things." Alan had simply turned away and entered Lamont Hall, where he taught his class, leaving her to sort out her tangled loyalties. He had no right to pick on her, question her that way. Why should she have to defend herself to him or anyone else?

And yet today she had felt an odd quickening as she hurried out of her Psych class to see if he was waiting for her as usual. He was on the steps eating a chocolate bar. "I saved half for you," he said, proffering it in lieu of an apology.

"Alan, you weren't very nice yesterday," she said, determined not to let the whole episode pass.

"Who ever said I was nice?" Alan took her book bag, and put his arm around her shoulder. "The Boat Pond?"

She nodded, slipped off her sandals, and they walked along slowly together. She felt very slight walking beside him. Beneath her feet, the lush grass felt moist and giving. She curled her toes into it with each step. "Alan, I was thinking about what you said, about the napalm and all that. Roy didn't fly a bomber, he flew reconnaissance." Alan opened his mouth to protest. She shoved the rest of the chocolate bar into it. "Okay, okay, don't say it. But Alan, if you look at it the way you do, everybody over there is a war criminal except the clerk-typists."

Alan swallowed the chocolate. "Why leave them out?"

Ever since Roy had gone down, Sandy had experienced only sympathy from people she met. They soothed her and tried in every way not to upset her. Except for Alan.

Alan was kind, she decided, but he wasn't sympathetic. The combination was bracing and profoundly disturbing.

Sandy looked down at Alan, who had fallen asleep, one arm clutched around his chest, the other flung out at an odd angle reminding her of a wounded soldier. The air felt suddenly chill, and as she stared down at him, she felt a flash of fear stronger and more unreasonable than any she had felt since Roy left.

"Dear Roy, I have decided to go back to school. . . ." She crumpled up the black-edged seven-line form and reached for another.

"Dear Roy, How are you, my darling? I miss you. Hey, guess what? I decided to go back to school. I thought it would be good for me. . . ." Why the hell was she writing about what was good for *her?* She crumpled this sheet too, and dropped it into the straw wastebasket by the side of the card table. Maybe it didn't matter what she wrote or how she worded it. All this fuss and attention to his feelings. Perhaps he no longer existed and she might just as well have sent the first letter, blunt and informational. But if he was alive, then every word was important; she must convey just the right feeling to him.

Sandy went over to her dresser. From the mirror above it she pulled out the snapshot of Roy and his buddy Steve in their flight suits and beneath it the color photo of Roy and her, arms draped around each other's bare skins in their bathing suits ("C'mon, let's make it sexy," Steve had goaded them before he snapped it). She laid them down on the card table and stared hard at the wavy-haired, clean-shaven boy she had married. She *had* to believe he was alive. In order to write to him, she had to imagine him alive before her or sitting on the hard bunk of a North Vietnamese prison camp thinking of her. She closed her eyes and held his face before her for a moment. Then she picked up the pen and began to print.

Dear Roy,
    How are you, my darling? I am well, but I miss you. Our poodle still keeps me company. When you come back we'll get a real dog. I got tired of my job at the bank, so I decided to go back to school to study to be a teacher. So far it's real interesting and keeps me busy. Come back to me soon. All my love,
                                                    Sandy

She reread it quickly, closed the self-sealing envelope, padded out into the hall in her slippers, and watched as the tissue-paper letter fell silently into the blackness of the building's mail chute.

Usually Sandy looked forward to the long drive to Chester. She loved to speed along the freeway, her arm out the window, singing along with the car radio, surrendering herself to the illusion that there was some momentum in her life, that she was going some place. This morning she kept both hands on the wheel as though any loss of control might also cause her determination to slacken and go limp—for she felt with equal intensity that what she intended to ask of Colonel Lloyd was as dishonorable as it was necessary.

Sandy planned to ask Colonel Lloyd to let her go. She wanted the United States Air Force to declare Roy Lawton—her husband of two weeks, of whom she had had no word in the twenty-seven months since he had been shot down and disappeared into the jungles of a faraway land, of whom her few recollections had by now drifted away like lovely but perishable soap bubbles—to declare this man dead.

For in truth, she thought he was. Unlike Fay, who communed with her missing husband, or Sharon Dornbeck, who felt, who absolutely *knew* Richard was there, Sandy had nothing, no dreams, no hunches, no middle-of-the-night flashes that Roy was alive, breathing, moving flesh and blood. Once she had confided to Mary Kaye that she could hardly remember Roy, and Mary Kaye had shrugged, "Everybody goes through that, don't worry about it," the implication being that it would pass. It hadn't passed. And now Sandy wanted someone to release the bonds that locked her to a man probably dead, someone to let her out of the limbo of the last two years.

Smitty waved to Sandy from his guard booth as she pulled into the base. The rest of Florida seemed to change constantly, she thought, old landmarks falling, new ones sprouting in response to a shifting population. Chester's population was constantly changing too; yet Chester itself never seemed to change. She passed the same pink-rollered women on their way to the PX, sleeveless blouses hanging outside their Bermuda shorts; the same clusters of men walking along briskly in their Air Force blues; the same low brick rectangles of junior officers' quarters, one of which had been home to her and Roy. It was all the same as she remembered it; only she herself seemed different.

The choice of reading material in the waiting room outside Colonel Lloyd's office was as meager as ever: two back issues of *Commander's Digest* and three of *Sports Illustrated*. She sat on the cracked green leather couch, her legs crossed demurely under her brown tweed jumper, and played with Fifi, the name she had given to the tiny ballerina who danced on a hoop suspended from a pearl bracelet. The bracelet, a gift from her father on her sixteenth birthday, was her lucky charm. She loved the dainty little dancer in her eighteenth-century costume, one toe pointed gracefully up behind her dress, doomed never to finish her pirouette. Fifi was the subject of the only composition on which she had ever received an A. Her English teacher had written, "A charming poignant story —but watch punctuation." Sandy still had the composition pasted in her high-school memory book. After Fifi brought her the A, Sandy always wore her on important occasions, when she needed luck.

At exactly ten o'clock, a buzzer sounded on Sergeant Bascomb's desk, the signal that Colonel Lloyd was ready to see her. The military being one of the last bastions of old-fashioned courtesies, the sergeant opened the door for her, announcing "Mrs. Lawton, sir." Colonel Lloyd looked up from his paperwork when she entered, stood and clasped both hands around hers, a big smile stretching across his tanned, healthy face. "Well, Sandy, how nice to see you. I was beginning to think you were high-hatting us. We missed you at the film ID last month."

She sat down in the brown leather chair across from his desk. "I've been kind of busy. I'm back at school."

He lowered his trim form into the swivel-back chair. "I *did* hear that, come to think of it. How do you like hitting the books again?"

"Oh, very much."

"Good for you!" Colonel Lloyd picked up some manila folders on his desk, opened a drawer and began carefully filing away the folders as he talked to her. "You meet some nice young people?"

Sandy glanced at him sharply. He slipped the last folder in just the right slot, unaware that his remark had any special meaning for Sandy, and looked up at her, pleased with himself for having finished his task, pleased too at what he considered his deft handling of a primary next of kin. "Now," he smiled at her, "tell me what's on your mind."

"Well, Colonel Lloyd," Sandy began, keeping her eyes down on the lucite handle of her tortoise-shell pocketbook, "I was wondering . . . under what conditions you people make a Killed in Action determination?" Not until she got through the question did she look at him.

He leaned back in his chair, clasping his hands behind his head. "When we have concrete evidence that a man has been killed in action." He eyed her levelly.

"Yes, but sometimes, even if you don't find a body . . ." Sandy paused and looked at him anxiously.

"Oh, I see what you mean." Colonel Lloyd swung himself forward, planted his right elbow on the desk and made his hand into a fist. "One," his thumb snapped up, "we accept an eyewitness report on the ground, from a fellow crew member who reports seeing the deceased body. Two," another finger popped up, "aerial ID. Sometimes the boys in the choppers fly low enough to verify a death —but that's pretty unusual. And three," a third finger joined the other two, "we can make dental IDs if we find the deceased's teeth."

Sandy nodded and began playing with the handle of her pocketbook. She shifted her position in the chair. She felt utterly unable to speak plainly to this man lest he judge her.

"Now, Sandy, I know what you're worried about." She looked gratefully toward him, as he leaned forward in his chair closer to her. "We won't make a KIA determination for Roy. We can't. We have to have some specific proof. That's always been our policy." His hands moved through the air as he spoke, reassuring, as though to brush away her fears. "Nobody is going to declare your husband dead. You can relax on that score."

Sandy forced herself to speak. "But you don't have any proof that he's alive either."

"No."

"And someone like Jane York, Earl's been missing longer than Roy, but his squadron leader was in communication with him after he landed, so Jane knows Earl at least survived the impact. I don't have anything like that to go on." Would he think she was dreadful for doubting that Roy was alive, she wondered. Would he even tell her if he thought Roy was dead?

"Sandy," he looked at her almost paternally, "there is absolutely no reason to believe Roy is dead. Roy is missing." He paused as if that word had clarified some point, then stood up. He walked her to the door, one arm draped casually around her shoulder, his head bent low like a football coach talking urgently to a valued player, trying to give him confidence. "Until there's a cessation of hostilities over there—even if it takes ten more years—or unless we have specific proof to the contrary, we will carry Roy as MIA." He turned to her in the doorway and smiled kindly. "Feel better?"

She nodded, managed a quick smile, and fled the Casualty Office and Chester Air Force Base. There were no answers.

Sergeant Vinza poked his head in the door. "Was that Mrs. Lawton?"

"Yes, it was."

"Gee, I'm sorry, Colonel Lloyd. I didn't know she was coming in."

"That's okay, Tony, I took care of it." Lloyd reached for his felt-tipped pen and began initialing memos. "She wanted us to declare her husband KIA."

"Jesus, another one?" Tony shook his head in disbelief.

12

American Prisoners of War and Missing in
Action in Southeast Asia (as of May 6, 1971)

By Country:

	MISSING	CAPTURED	TOTAL
NVN	406	378	784
SVN	501	79	580
LAOS	263	3	266
TOTAL	1170	460	1630

By Service:

	MISSING	CAPTURED	TOTAL
Army	408	59	467
Navy	108	143	251
Marine Corps	93	23	116
Air Force	561	235	796
TOTAL	1170	460	1630

They had stopped for a few moments in Alan's apartment
on their way out to dinner. She had asked to see an article
he had written, and he was rummaging through the papers
on his desk, trying to find it. "I don't know where it is," he
said, continuing to search.

"Well, keep looking, I really want to see it." Alan's
apartment, she immediately sensed, was a world different
in its names and sounds and objects from any she was
used to. On the stereo, classical music was playing. The

clear, precise notes of a flute filled the room. Her eyes
flickered around. Cracked, yellow-beige walls and a poster
of children playing idyllically on a hillside. Above it the
suggestion, GIVE PEACE A CHANCE. A shiny-surfaced re-
production, showing a tall, bluish man with a smaller
figure on his side, tilted loosely in its frame toward a felt
pennant proclaiming HOBART. Stuck around the letters
was a collection of buttons, DUMP JOHNSON, WE TRY
HARDER, LOVE, I SHOULD HAVE STAYED IN BED, SUP-
PORT GUN LEGISLATION. Books and papers were not confined to the room's official bookcase, a row of plywood
boards stretched across two piles of bricks. They also lay
scattered across Alan's chipped mahogany desk and rose
in fraying paper towers above his two hi-fi speakers.

She picked up a large instrument lying on a table near
the stereo. "What's this?"

"A bass recorder." Carefully she laid it down again.

His apartment felt small and foreign to her. A faded
brown-plaid bedspread and curtains, well-worn refugees
from years of academia, were the only coordinated ele-
ments. Like its occupant, the room's combination of homi-
ness and eclecticism seemed exotic to Sandy, comfortable
yet unpredictable. She thought of the barren walls and
hastily chosen furniture in her apartment, by comparison
with his, as undefined and impersonal as a motel room
on a turnpike.

"Here, I found it." Alan pulled out a dusty green
journal from a shelf near his desk. "If you really want to
see it," he looked at her dubiously, "it's on page thirty-
three."

She grabbed the journal from him and opened it.
" 'Color Coding and Reading Quotients, by Alan Webber,' " she read out loud. Her eye fell to the small-print
biography at the bottom of the page. " 'Alan Webber is
an instructor in Early Childhood Education at Walton
State College.' Oh, Alan!" She looked up at him, reverent
and impressed.

"Sandy, it's a nothing journal. It probably has a circu-
lation of thirty-two or something."

"But to write something, to see your name in print like that! Can I borrow it?"

He shrugged his shoulders, more touched than he would admit. "You can keep it. I've got another copy." She put it next to her purse and sat in a straw basket-chair under a NO LOITERING sign. Alan was perched on the edge of the double bed, across the room from her, listening to the music. "You know, I heard Rampal play this once in New York," he said.

"Who?"

"Jean-Pierre Rampal. He's the famous French flutist."

"Oh. What's the name of the piece?" she inquired.

"The name of the *piece*," he laughed, "is the B minor Flute Sonata, by Bach."

"I'm not too familiar with classical music."

"You don't say," he teased her.

"I should probably take a music-appreciation course," she said, hating him for making her feel foolish.

"Good idea. I'll give it to you."

The bathroom door was open. On the inside hook hung a maroon robe, and next to it the bottoms of a pair of light blue pajamas. She felt Alan watching her, and the room suddenly seemed very small to her. "Hey," she said, "shouldn't we be getting on to dinner?"

He reached over to his desk and picked up a gray paper bag which she had noticed lying there. "Here." He walked over and held it out to her, his voice slightly gruff. "Open it. It's for you."

She looked at him with surprise. Slowly she opened the bag, reached in and lifted out a pale, rosy-pink Pakistani shirt, embroidered all over in mauve and green. Around its collarless neck was a row of tiny round mirrors. She held it up against herself, looking down at it. "They only come in two sizes," she heard Alan saying, "so I thought the smaller. . . ." He hesitated, "You don't like it, do you?"

She looked up at him, and the tears spilled out of her eyes, dripping down onto the delicately colored shirt. "It just . . . Alan, it just knocks me out!"

She was crying, and his arms were around her, holding

her tenderly. His lips brushed over her eyes, and she felt the pleasant scratchiness of his beard against her face. Suddenly her loneliness, the uncertainty of the last two years, the closeness of the room, and her own need all unleashed a physical longing in her so intense that she experienced it first almost as a wave of nausea. The shirt dropped to the floor, and she moaned as she felt the thrust of his tongue.

His control drove her almost wild, and as they made love, ardently and lengthily, the late afternoon blending into evening, the last thing on Sandy's mind was a young man who might or might not be alive in Indochina.

13

Letter from the Department of the Air Force

Dear Air Force Next of Kin,

The Fairchild Hiller Corporation is deeply concerned over the plight of American personnel who are missing in action or captured in Southeast Asia and their families back home. Resulting from its desire to be of assistance, the company is making the attached greeting card, with enclosure, available to all next of kin to be sent to their relatives, friends and acquaintances in conjunction with the forthcoming holiday season. If you are interested, you may obtain, free of charge, as many copies of the card as you desire by writing to the Public Relations Office, Fairchild Hiller Corporation, Germantown, Maryland 20767. This does not constitute an official endorsement of that firm by the Department of the Air Force or any other agency of the government. . . .

"Open the door and let me in."
"Not by the hair on my chinny-chin chin."
"Then I'll huff and puff and I'll blow your house in!"
Huff! Puff! A balding Kiwanian crouched behind the

blue velvet curtain of the tiny puppet theater, puffed out his cheeks and bellowed forth air with all his might. With each puff he moved the wolf's head closer to the pigs' cardboard-brick door. "Eeee," he raised his voice to a falsetto, imitating the panic of the little pigs inside and was rewarded by shrieks of terror and delight from the children in the audience.

"See the puppets, Timmy?" Diane Devere whispered to her eighteen-month-old, seated on her lap sucking a candy cane. Timmy switched the candy cane to his other hand, wiping his sticky hand on his starched jump suit, and watched the wolf climb up on the roof of the pigs' house. Diane gave a quick glance to check her one-month-old slumbering in a detachable car-bed underneath the punch and cookie table. Pretty, she thought. Jim always wanted a girl. That morning Diane had mailed off three copies of the hospital birth photo: one to Laos, where Jim was supposed to have gone down, one to North Vietnam, and one to Communist China, just in case he had strayed. She wondered how long it would be before the photos of their daughter came back, the envelopes stamped ADDRESSEE UNKNOWN.

Kim Hochart, dressed in a red velvet smock dress and black patent-leather party shoes, stood up, clasping her hands together, to get a better view of the wolf's debacle. Billy and Jamie Holroyd, dressed in identical short pants, white shirts, and bow ties, crouched Indian-fashion on the floor, oblivious to the fact that their blue high socks had fallen down again. Kathy and Julie Buell watched the show with their arms around their knees, open-mouthed. Their brothers stood back, embarrassed to be looking at kiddie entertainment but clearly not uninterested.

A large blue-and-gold Kiwanis banner was tacked on one wall of the spacious meeting hall. Next to it was a blown-up photograph of an emaciated prisoner of war, dressed in rags and naked from the waist up, mouth open and knees drawn up like the children watching the puppet show, seated on a wooden slab staring into space. Over this, on a piece of white posterboard, was inked the reassurance, KIWANIS CARES. The lights from the spreading

Christmas tree blinked on and off under the poster, casting cheerful reflections on the photograph of the prisoner's cell. A large cut-out of Rudolph the Red-Nosed Reindeer was hung on the opposite wall, and red and green streamers strung with candy canes were looped above his head. In the rest of the room, the families of the POWs and MIAs moved around, carefully avoiding the wires and television cables strewn about. Mingling with the women were Kiwanians, gold K's gleaming in their lapels, party hats on their heads. An atmosphere of determined good cheer prevailed.

Mary Kaye Buell and Margaret Holroyd were standing in a corner watching the festivities. A blustery-faced man, with a shock of gray hair peeking out from beneath his gold paper hat, approached them, a hearty smile plastered on his face. "Can I bring you ladies some punch?"

"Thanks very much." Mary Kaye's voice assumed its bouncy, exaggeratedly sweet tone, and Margaret sensed trouble. "Say," Mary Kaye continued brightly, "I wonder how in the world the media heard about this Christmas party?" She beamed at the Kiwanian.

"Oh, we called 'em," he announced proudly. Then, bending forward, in a low tone of camaraderie, he added, "We knew this would make a good human-interest story."

"You fellas sure are on your toes," Mary Kaye said sweetly. The Kiwanian smiled at the compliment. "I'll bring you a plate of cookies too," he said gallantly, and Mary Kaye and Margaret watched him head for the refreshment table.

"I know they're trying to be nice," Margaret said, taking in the room's tinselly cheer, "but they treat us like we're pitiful freaks or something."

Mary Kaye sighed. "Don't fret, Margaret." She watched the Kiwanian smilingly make his way back toward them, a cup of punch in each hand and a plate of cookies and cakes balanced between. "We're just their good works for December. Next month they'll move on to Cerebral Palsy." Margaret smiled and accepted the punch glass, grateful that the man had not overheard Mary Kaye. Margaret hated scenes.

The puppet show was over, and a Kiwanian covered with a white cotton beard and padded Santa Claus suit entered the room and pranced over to the Christmas tree. "Come right over here, kids," he boomed out, laying a large sack filled with packages down on the floor. Padding and all, he settled himself into a black metal bridge chair. "I have a present in this bag for every child, so don't crowd. Just wait until your name is called." The children rushed over and seated themselves on the floor around Santa Claus's feet, eagerly waiting. Santa reached into his bag, pulled out a present and, holding the tag at arm's length, read with difficulty, "Billy Holroyd." Amy Holroyd gave her brother a push. "Go on!" Billy had suddenly become shy. "Billy, go on! Don't you want your present?" Billy shuffled up and grabbed the package, eyes down. A murmur of approval ran through the audience, and then Margaret's voice, "Billy, what do you say?" Billy, already back in his seat, muttered, "Thank you," and everyone chuckled appreciatively.

"Is there a young lady named Kim Hochart?" Santa was holding up a rectangular package. Kim smiled broadly and hurried over to Santa. "Thank you, Santa." She curtsied, her long blond hair looking almost white against the red velvet dress.

"Hold it, can we get a picture here, Mike?" a young television reporter called to his cameraman. "Santa, can you pick her up?"

Santa picked up Kim and put her on his lap. She blinked innocently at the cameras. "Should she be holding her present?" Santa inquired of the reporter. "Looks like a doll."

"Yeah, that's good." The reporter nodded.

"Kim," Santa said, already pulling off the wrapping from the present, "let's open it up and then the man will take our picture." It was a Barbie Doll, and Santa took it out of its box. Another Kiwanian rushed to retrieve the paper and box and crumpled them up, safely out of the camera's way.

"Kim," the cameraman called, "will you kiss Santa Claus?" The little girl obediently held the doll in her arms and kissed Santa's cottony cheek. "Good, good. Now, once more." The cameras rolled, and Jojo Hochart, standing with a group of mothers, looked on happily.

Oh, well, Mary Kaye thought to herself, publicity is publicity. She didn't mind a little exploitation for a good cause. She bit into a jelly doughnut the Kiwanian had brought her. For the first two years Brian was away, Mary Kaye had been careful about her weight. That was because she expected Brian home at any moment. She even continued the birth control pills which she had had to overcome her Catholic scruples to take after the arrival of their fourth child. Mary Kaye wiped the jelly from around her mouth. Her black-and-white silk printed dress felt tight around her waist. By the third year she had lost her illusions, gone off the pill, indulged all her food fancies, and comforted herself with the promise that with the first serious talk of releasing the prisoners, she would go on a diet. If there was one thing she had learned from the years of waiting, it was that diplomacy moved slowly; she figured she would have plenty of time to get thin.

Ricky Dornbeck, Sharon's five-year-old, ran over to his mother holding a toy garage. "Sharon, look!" he said excitedly.

"Oh, Ricky, how wonderful!" his mother said.

"I'm gonna ask Daddy to help me put it together tonight," he said earnestly and ran off to show it to someone else. Diane Devere and Jane York, standing near Sharon, looked at her, the question on their faces. "He keeps callin' my Dad 'Daddy,'" Sharon explained. "I keep tellin' him not to. . . ." She raised her hands helplessly.

Underneath the KIWANIS CARES sign, Pete Buell was being interviewed. He wore a sport jacket, and his hair was combed and his face unusually clean in the glare of the bright lights. A microphone was shoved in front of his mouth. "Peter, how old are you?" the reporter's voice asked.

"Ten."

"Having a good time today?" The voice was cheerful.

"Sure."

"Peter, how long has your dad been in prison camp?"

"Four years," Peter said matter-of-factly.

"When he comes home, Peter, tell us, what are some of the things you'd like to do with him?"

Peter shrugged his shoulders. "Depends when he comes home." He looked toward the reporter, but the reporter said nothing, he only continued to hold the mike in front of Pete's face. The lights were still brightly on him. Pete realized that more was expected of him. "If he comes home next year," the boy continued, "I'd be eleven and I'd want to do certain things. If he comes home in five years, I'll be fifteen. You want to do different things when you're fifteen, I guess." The microphone did not move. "It depends when he comes home."

Atta boy, Pete! Mary Kaye silently cheered her son's answer to the pointless, insensitive question. He was so like his father, stubborn, sure of himself, irresistible. She watched him leave the microphone and join his brother. Finished with Peter Buell, the camera swung its focus to general footage—children playing with their presents; Santa Claus chatting with the mothers; a Kiwanian on all fours, party hat still on his head, giving two tow-headed children a ride on his back. Mary Kaye thought of her brother Kevin, who used to play surrogate father to her children, giving them pig-a-back rides and appearing at school conferences and Little League games until his wife, Joanne, politely but firmly told Mary Kaye that after all Kevin had his own children to attend to and wasn't Mary Kaye being a little selfish and unreasonable to count so much on Kevin? Ah, yes, Mary Kaye thought, someone could make a fortune starting a Rent-a-Father business.

In the corner Jane was talking to Sharon. "Did you hear, Mrs. Calafano got a letter from her son?"

"Oh, that is marvelous!" Sharon exclaimed. "He'd been missin' for more than two years, hadn't he?"

"That's right, but you know she didn't hear through the mails. Emily Brunner brought the letter back on her last trip from Hanoi."

"Emily Brunner!" In the Gundersen household, Emily Brunner was a bad word. Head of the local Peace and

Freedom Committee, she was known to traffic with Hanoi. Sharon had heard that Mrs. Brunner had been remarkably successful in getting mail and packages to prisoners and occasionally in bringing information back from North Vietnam. "I think Richard would rather not hear from me than get a package or letter via Emily Brunner's group," Sharon said. Jane looked at her skeptically.

"Say, could we get an interview with one of you wives, please?" The reporter walked over to Mary Kaye and several of the other women.

"Which one of us would you like?" Mary Kaye inquired sweetly. "As if I didn't know."

The reporter looked around slowly, giving the impression of making a difficult but necessary choice. "How about the lady in the blue dress over there?" He nodded his head to the left. Sharon Dornbeck tapped her chest— me?—smiled sweetly, and excused herself from the others. She stood beside the microphone, smoothing the imaginary disarray of her blond hair, and smiled out at the camera from beneath the poster of a scrawny, half-naked POW.

Men are all the same, Mary Kaye thought. They always pick the prettiest one. She took another jelly doughnut off the paper plate and resolutely sank her teeth into it.

When she got home after the party, a large florist's box was propping open the storm door. She carried the package into the kitchen and unwrapped a brilliantly colored poinsettia plant. From one stalk a gold-lettered card hung down. "Peace on Earth, Good Will to Men. Best Wishes from the President and His Family."

Mary Kaye put the plant back into the box, pressed her foot on the garbage can lever, and carefully dropped the President's present inside.

14

Letter from the Department of the Air Force

Dear Air Force Next of Kin,

North Vietnam stated that it would provide
information about American prisoners
through the so-called New Mobilization Committee in this country. We cannot endorse
this or similar groups nor their use by North
Vietnamese to further political objectives,
especially at your expense. However, we will
take no action to impede the flow of information about our personnel, and you will be
kept apprised of all developments. We, in
turn, would appreciate your immediately
notifying us of any additional information
that may be made available to you regarding
your relative in the event this occurs.

It is clear that as of the present time no
information concerning the status of any
missing or captured personnel has been
furnished these groups.

As to what actions the families should take,
you must be governed by the dictates of
your own conscience. Of course, you should
not provide these groups with information

which has been furnished to you on a personal, privileged basis by the Air Force. We
recommend name, grade, and service number at time of loss, date of birth, and date
and country of loss (Southeast Asia in the
case of Laos); also, a photo of the member
may be included if desired. You should
immediately report to us any attempt to
coerce or intimidate you into taking action
which might be contrary to your best interests, or those of our missing and captured
servicemen, or your country.

When Sharon Dornbeck decided to visit Emily Brunner
at the Gulf Area Peace and Freedom Committee, she felt
there was no point in telling her father. He would disap-
prove, she knew, and after defying him once and going
to Paris, she felt unable to cope with another argument,
or worse yet, his silent, wounded displeasure. Sharon disagreed with Emily Brunner politically, But it was already
January, the start of a new year, seven months since her
husband went down. After being buoyed up by her parents
all day and expressing her faith on public platforms that
her husband was still alive, Sharon was having trouble
sleeping. This month she packed her usual package for
Richard, the package which always came back three
months later marked NOT DELIVERABLE, and instead of
taking it to her post office as usual, parked her car in
front of the run-down third-floor offices of the Gulf Area
Peace and Freedom Committee and carried it nervously
up the worn, wooden stairs. If she could get a package
through to Richard, if she could just find out if he was
alive, it would be worth it, she told herself; her father
would forgive her later.

Mrs. Brunner's office consisted of one large room, in
which everything looked second-hand—the dented filing
cabinet; the splintery wooden desks; a mimeograph
machine, an anachronism in the age of Xerography; and
a few Salvation Army chairs. On the walls were large,

blown-up pictures of anguished Vietnamese women, wailing silently into the lens of the camera, before the bodies of their children. Sharon quickly looked away. A well-dressed, middle-aged volunteer who looked as if she should have been out on the links was stuffing letters into envelopes. Mrs. Brunner herself was on the phone, a pencil stuck into her graying hair, which was pulled back into a bun. She gestured with her thick, black-framed glasses as she talked rapidly and precisely. "Yes," Emily Brunner was saying, "our next group is going to Hanoi in about ten days. Yes, of course, we're carrying mail. No, we never know if we'll be able to deliver it until we get there. . . ." Without missing a beat in her conversation, she looked up and motioned Sharon over to a chair in front of her desk. It wasn't an invitation; it was an order. "Yes, one of our wives is here right now with a package for her husband. . . ." She looked at Sharon questioningly; Sharon nodded. "No, I'm sorry," Mrs. Brunner continued, "I'm really too busy for any more interviews. . . . Oh, all right. Wednesday at two-thirty. Make sure your man is here on the dot. Wednesdays are very bad for me. Yes, all right, good-by." She hung up the phone. "Don't these media people drive you crazy?" she smiled at Sharon, girl-to-girl. "Now let's see, what can I help you with? A package for your husband?" She pulled the package across the desk and glanced at the name. "You're new here. MIA?" Sharon nodded. "Any questions, Mrs. Dornbeck?" Mrs. Brunner eyed her curiously.

"Well," Sharon began nervously, "I just was hopin' maybe you could tell me somethin' about my husband." Sharon ended all her sentences with her voice up in the air, which made everything she said sound like a question. "He's been missin' over seven months. I put everythin' in the package you suggested," Sharon continued. "The only thing is, I didn't quite understand about the thermal underwear."

"I'm sure we had thermal underwear on the list," Mrs. Brunner said, yanking open her desk drawer with difficulty. "I'd give my soul for a decent piece of furniture around here. There." She pulled a stenciled list from the

drawer. "Thermal underwear. It is perfectly acceptable."
She smiled across at Sharon.

"I know it's on the list," Sharon said, "but . . ."

"If it's on the list, Mrs. Dornbeck, it means the authorities in Hanoi have okayed it. We didn't make up the list."
Mrs. Brunner put the list back in her drawer which she
jammed shut again.

"I know, but it seems so strange."

"Why, may I ask?"

"Well," Sharon smiled engagingly, "it's so hot over
there, all those rice paddies 'n' everythin'."

"That's *South* Vietnam, Mrs. Dornbeck," Emily Brunner explained like a teacher talking to a retarded child.
"Your husband is missing over *North* Vietnam."

Another one, Emily Brunner thought, another Bible-belt, bouffant-haired wife expecting sympathy while she
lived on her husband's paycheck, with only the dimmest
notion of the geography of Vietnam and probably less
notion of the war's politics.

The well-to-do wife of a Tampa industrialist, Emily
Brunner had long been active in the peace movement, a
daring pursuit in a politically conservative community
dominated by a military base. Not only did she organize
the local priests, ministers, and rabbis into a Committee
of Concerned Clergy (though she herself was an atheist);
she also persuaded area artists to donate paintings and
sculptures which were then auctioned off in an affair successful beyond her wildest dreams. There were not enough
tickets for all the people who wanted to buy for peace.

The Gulf Area Peace and Freedom Committee linked
up with several other peace groups throughout the land
in seizing on the POW/MIA issue. In a series of dramatic
trips to Hanoi, arranged through certain Washington connections, Emily Brunner's group had succeeded in becoming an unofficial and reliable conduit for mail and
packages between prisoners in North Vietnam and their
families in the Tampa area. The POW/MIA question
attracted Emily Brunner particularly because it was both
emotional and nonpartisan. As such, Mrs. Brunner felt

that championing it would attract new adherents to the peace movement. Besides, she did feel some sympathy for the women, though God knows the ones to feel sympathy for, she reminded herself every now and again, were the boys who were shipped home in green bags, not these women who drew up to her office in station wagons.

"By the way, Mrs. Dornbeck, have you seen this article?" She handed Sharon a reprint entitled "POW Families: Pawns of the Administration."

"No." Sharon smiled.

"Well, why don't you take it?"

"All right." She folded it and put it into her purse.

"I'll be interested in hearing what you think of it."

Mrs. Brunner's soft-sell crusade was beginning to annoy Sharon. She forced herself to smile. "Well, you know I'm not a political person."

"Is that a slogan with you wives?" Mrs. Brunner didn't even bother to mask her irritation. She stood up, signaling that the meeting was over. "I'll be sure to let you know if I can find out anything about your husband. By the way," she added, "I hope you didn't make the usual mistake of getting the thermal underwear three sizes smaller, assuming your husband is down to skin and bones."

"Well, I do understand, from what the few released prisoners have said, that the food isn't too good over there."

"There are always a few people who complain," Mrs. Brunner said patiently, "but all the peace groups have found that the men are being very well treated."

"I sure hope so." Was Mrs. Brunner right? Sharon wondered. She thought of the stories she had read of men being given squash soup and rice and of pictures published in the paper of stick-thin prisoners. But Mrs. Brunner should know; her group had been in Hanoi. Another instance of conflicting information. Why was nothing clear in this war?

"A rice-based diet is the healthiest thing in the world," Mrs. Brunner assured Sharon, walking her to the door. "Have you ever seen a fat Vietnamese?"

Three nights later, as Sharon was sitting with her parents having a cup of coffee in the living room and Ricky was watching television, the doorbell rang. She went to answer it.

"Mrs. Sharon Dornbeck?"

"I'm Mrs. Dornbeck." A middle-aged man in a gray suit, overly narrow black tie, and instantly forgettable face stood outside.

"My name is Bob Jones. I'm with the Federal Bureau of Investigation." He opened a leather case containing a card.

"The FBI?" Sharon felt suddenly guilty.

"Who is it, Sharon?" her father called. "If someone's there, invite 'em inside."

She showed Mr. Jones to a chair. "These are my parents, Colonel and Mrs. Gundersen. This gentleman's from the FBI."

"Mrs. Dornbeck," Bob Jones began. He glanced at Paula and Jerry Gundersen. "I assume I can speak freely." Sharon nodded. "Mrs. Dornbeck, we at the Bureau have been keeping an eye on some of the local peace groups and watching their connections to the families of the men missing in Vietnam. In that regard, I don't suppose by any chance you've had any contact with those groups?" He looked at her blandly, as if it were the most natural question in the world.

"I can tell you my daughter certainly hasn't had anything to do with the peace groups," Jerry Gundersen said firmly.

Sharon had the feeling this was all taking place in a dream.

"Yes," she said softly, not looking at her father, "I did see Emily Brunner a few days ago. I gave her a package to take to my husband."

"You WHAT?" Jerry exploded.

"Sh, Jerry." Paula put her hand on her husband's arm.

"They didn't by any chance give you any literature, did they, Mrs. Dornbeck?" Bob Jones asked. As her father watched, astonished, Sharon nodded meekly. "We'd like to examine what it is they're passing out." Sharon walked over to her purse, pulled out the reprinted article, and silently handed it over to Bob Jones. "Thanks so much, Mrs. Dornbeck. Sorry to trouble you people." Mr. Jones got up. "I'll be sure to send this back to you when I'm done."

"No need to do that," Jerry said decisively, escorting Mr. Jones to the door and glancing angrily at his daughter. "Glad to see you fellas are on the job."

Sharon sat quietly with her head in her hands. She remembered the time she had been caught putting a red hair ribbon into her pocket at the five-and-ten-cent store. The store manager and her parents had all looked at her so shocked and disappointed. She had wanted to tell them that it was all right, she had only seen something pretty and she hadn't wanted to ask them for money; she wasn't a *bad* person.

Her father was looking at her like that now. Underneath she felt angry at Mrs. Brunner, angry at the FBI man, even angry at her father. But since these were forbidden targets, Sharon picked a more permissible one. She felt furious with herself.

15

From an Air Force Base in Arizona

Dear Air Force Next of Kin,

It is the policy of the Air Force to contact Next-of-Kin of missing or captured service members every four to six weeks, more or less to insure you of our continued interest. It comes to mind now, however, that our letters say absolutely nothing unless we have new information to report to you. We are wondering if you would rather we continue sending you letters every four to six weeks or if maybe you would rather hear only when we have new news to report

Periodically, our headquarters at Randolph Air Force Base, Texas, sends you a news letter concerning the latest general information on missing or captured persons. By the time we get copies of the news letter you already have received it and anything we would report to you would be repetitious. We sincerely feel that sending letter after letter telling you we have no news is not appropriate.

One evening in early February, Mary Kaye mixed herself her usual bourbon and water, settled herself in the club chair and picked up the phone. "Operator, I'd like to make a collect call to Randolph Air Force Base, Department of Personnel Services, please." She lifted her drink and turned to her husband's photograph. "Ready for the evening's entertainment, Bri?" She winked at him and took a long sip of her drink.

"Colonel Cross, Personnel, speaking," the voice announced on the other end of the line.

"Well, hello, Colonel Cross. You haven't been on duty lately, I've missed you," Mary Kaye said in a lilting sardonic voice.

"Oh, it's you, Mrs. Buell," Colonel Cross said dully.

"Yes, indeedy it *is*," she continued sweetly. "You fellas recognize my voice by now. Now that's what I call progress."

"Anything I can do for you Mrs. Buell?" Colonel Cross inquired.

"Well, I hope so, Colonel, I really do. I haven't given up on the United States Air Force yet. Now, I received your letter dated 14 January in which you ask for a *recent* photograph of my husband, Captain Brian Buell."

"Correct. Photo Analysis requested it."

"Yes, well, here's the problem," Mary Kaye continued smoothly. "You may recall that my husband, Captain Brian Buell, has not been around recently. Sorry about that; I'd love to oblige you fellas." She paused for a moment. "Now I do have in the other room a ten-year-old boy named Peter who resembles his father. Would that help? I could send you his photo, perhaps in his Little League uniform? . . ."

At Randolph Air Force Base in Texas, Colonel Cross rolled his eyes toward the ceiling. "Forget it, Mrs. Buell. I'll tell Photo Analysis to make do with what they've got."

"You do that."

"Thanks for calling."

"My pleasure." Mary Kaye hung up the phone and winked at her husband's picture. Well, she thought, if the Air Force can't take care of the wives, the wives'll take care of the Air Force. She finished her drink with a self-congratulatory air.

Pete, in mismated pajamas, came into the living room.

"He took a bath, will wonders never cease?" Mary Kaye said sardonically. "You clean the ring?"

"I'm going to right now. Can I watch *F Troop?*"

"You finish your homework?"

"Sort of."

"Yes or no?"

"I can finish it during the ads," Pete offered.

"Negative."

"Oh, Mom." Pete curled his toes around a stray pencil on the floor, lifted his foot and deposited the pencil on the coffee table. Mary Kaye suppressed a smile. This kid, who refused to learn to read properly, who drove her quietly crazy with his antics, was her favorite, the most like his father.

"Pete, look at me. You look more like Daddy every day, you know it?"

"That's what Aunt Marion said."

"She did?" Mary Kaye asked, pleased. "What did she say?"

"That I look a lot like Daddy."

"That's a compliment," his mother informed him. "Daddy's a very good-looking man."

Pete shrugged, embarrassed by the discussion of looks.

"Okay, mister, scoot."

Pete disappeared and Mary Kaye contemplated the evening ahead. She wanted to call Sandy to check on the latest developments between her and Alan. And she'd promised to call Margaret Holroyd, who was actively involved in forming a National Association of POW/MIA Relatives and was already planning a spring meeting in Chicago. Would Mary Kaye help? Yes, she thought, I'll help; I always do.

The girls were bedded down, Pete was accounted for, but she hadn't seen Joe since dinner. She walked upstairs and knocked on his door. Opening it, she took in at a glance the floor strewn with model airplane parts, pieces from his Battleship game, stamps, geodes, and broken

colored pencils. Joe was slumped in his black vinyl armchair looking up at her suspiciously. What the hell, she
thought, he's eleven years old. She sat down on a corner
of his corduroy spread. "I came to see how you were getting along with your homework."

"Okay," he muttered.

"Still on myths?" she asked brightly. "I used to love
those when I was a kid, all the gods and goddesses and
their heroic feats."

"I think they're stupid."

"Why, Joe?"

"Too unbelievable."

"But they're supposed to be like that. They aren't real,
they're—myths."

"They're still stupid."

Mary Kaye felt an unreasoning wave of annoyance. Joe
was so damned contrary. If she had hated myths, he
would have defended them. He took a superball from his
pocket and bounced it hard. It rebounded at an angle,
barely missing his new lamp. Piled on the desk, his
schoolbooks lay unopened. On the bed, not quite hidden
by the pillow, was the tip of a *Zorro* comic.

"Okay, Joe," she held out her hand, "I'll take the
comic."

"You don't have to take it, I won't read it."

"Give it to me." Sullenly, Joe walked to the bed, pulled
it out and handed it to her. "Joe, do I have to go over
it again? You don't read comics until you finish your
homework. You know the rules around here."

"Yeah, well, that's a stupid rule."

"Don't get fresh with me, buster! And quit calling
everything stupid." Joe stood with his hands jammed in
his dungaree pockets, kicking the post of the bed with
one sneakered foot. "You never clean up your room any
more."

"I would if you'd just give me a chance!"

"You've had a million chances! I'm sick of excuses and
I'm sick of your lazy sullen attitude! If you won't tell me
what's bugging you, at least shape up!" Mary Kaye looked
at her first-born, so remote and unreasonable. Joe had

taught himself to read in kindergarten and had astonished his parents with his quickness. "That one'll be ready for college when he's ten years old," Brian used to joke proudly. Mary Kaye's face softened. "Joey, I wish your father were here. Maybe he'd get along with you better than I seem to."

"Why don't you stop it?" Joe suddenly yelled at her, tears coursing down his cheeks. "Why don't you stop all this pretending about how great everything's gonna be when Dad comes home? I know what happened between you and Dad before he left! I heard it all! I know all about it!" He stared at her, defiant through his tears, then strode out of the room, slamming the door behind him with such force that the heap of parts to his DC-8 went flying under the bed.

Weakly, Mary Kaye stayed where she was, too stunned to think. Minutes later, her hands were still shaking as she automatically bent over and began picking up the pieces.

16

Letter from the Department of the Air Force

Dear Air Force Next of Kin,

On 12 December 1969, President and Mrs. Nixon met in the White House with twenty-one wives and five mothers of Air Force, Navy, Marine, and Army members who are missing in action or captured in North Vietnam, South Vietnam, and Laos. The President and First Lady would like to have met with all of the families, but obviously that was not practical. Final selections were made by the White House, and both enlisted personnel and officers were represented. You will be interested to know that nine Air Force wives attended the session.

President Nixon assured the wives and mothers that the prisoner problem will continue to receive the highest priority within his Administration. He stated that our government will do everything possible to have the prisoner-of-war issue handled on a humane basis apart from the political and military issues of the war itself. The President remarked that, while there are those who disagree with his Plan for Peace in Vietnam,

the subject of proper treatment and release
of prisoners of war is one on which all
Americans should be united. He indicated
further that there would be no precipitous
withdrawal which could leave the prisoner
issue unresolved, noting that such a withdrawal would also endanger the lives of
thousands of South Vietnamese as well as
imperil the security of remaining US forces.
President Nixon expressed his deep respect
for the bravery of the hundreds of wives,
children, parents, and other relatives who
have now lived so long without knowing
whether their loved ones are dead or alive.

When Alan Webber had said that his father was a CPA
in Brooklyn, he left out something important, at least to
his father. Mr. Webber was indeed a certified public
accountant, but only because the Depression had rudely
shattered his dreams of being a college professor.

The Webbers both fancied themselves socialists—a
word they used advisedly and never to business clients—
socialists of a certain stripe, however. They believed in a
more equitable distribution of wealth and applauded the
Russian experiment. They also applauded the dishwasher
and the air conditioner, both of which they acquired and
which in no way meant that one did not espouse socialism
after all—merely that one was adjusting to the realities of
life in a not-as-yet socialist country. They put their left-
liberal beliefs into practice by buying an attached house on
a square of attached houses, each with a small patch of
backyard opening onto a communal courtyard. None of
the neighbors was allowed to put up fences or shrubbery
that would in any way impede the communal view. Even
when the Lutz children used her hedges as first base and
the Del Vecchios pulled up the struggling lawn and
installed a sunken barbecue pit, over which they held huge
winy parties for their Italian relatives, Mrs. Webber still
felt proud to live in what she called "a communal experi-

ment." She was pleased that her only child, Alan, was exposed to "all sorts of people."

They gave Alan music lessons on both the piano and recorder and quietly discouraged his interest in the guitar. For his birthday they gave him books and records, never the battery-operated toys which he craved. He went to art-appreciation classes at the Museum of Modern Art and, of course, to public school. When Alan turned out to be only an average student, they said, "It would be one thing if you had no ability, but you're so *bright. . . . Why* don't you apply yourself more?" So Alan grew up in Brooklyn, exposed to all the cultural niceties of life, nagged by the feeling that he was always in some way displeasing his parents.

When it came time for him to go to college, they insisted that he apply to Amherst and Trinity and carefully masked their disappointment when he got into Hobart. They were delighted when he wanted to go on for a Ph.D. in education: teaching, after all, was "worthwhile," thus how much more worthwhile teaching teachers to teach! They approved of his beard and felt comfortable with his radicalism. He read Fanon and Mao, but they always knew that their son would never get himself blown up making bombs.

They never interfered with his choice of girls. Race, politics, or religion was never an obstacle to his parents' liberal views. "As long as the girl is intelligent and interesting, we couldn't care less about her background," his mother told him frequently. Whenever his mother said "intelligent and interesting," a vision of a hairy-lipped, bespectacled female rose before Alan's eyes, clutching his arm tightly as his mother beamed down on them benignly. The trouble with his mother's predilections in women, Alan had the sense to realize, was that all the intelligent, intense girls he met found him less than satisfactory, extremely nice but intellectually tentative, whereas he found their brainy composure overwhelming and in the end boring: it left him no role.

What drew him so to Sandy, he later thought, was not just that she was pretty—old-fashioned "pretty," with exactly the kind of clean-scrubbed, blond good looks his mother would have called "vapid"—but that she was an intellectual virgin. She looked up to him, found him a repository of knowledge, and, he sensed, was afraid to appear ignorant before him in exactly the same way he used to fear cultural *gaffes* in the presence of the more brilliant girls he had dated.

After they began sleeping together, Sandy never talked about Roy, and Alan learned not to ask. Whatever her guilt, whatever her private anguish, she expressed none of it to him. Once, when she was lying quietly next to him, he thought he saw tears in her eyes and asked her what was the matter. "Nothing," she answered quickly and turned to him with a slight smile. Before he could probe further, she leaned over him and began kissing his ear, his mouth, running her hands along his body. The intensity of her passion amazed him. It was as if by her total concentration on making love to him, she was blotting out the shadow of anyone else. Or perhaps, he sometimes thought, she had merely decided that the risk of commitment was preferable to the safety of loneliness. In any event, she never mentioned her husband, and after a while, without ever saying anything about it to Sandy or even admitting it in words to himself, Alan began to assume that Roy was probably dead.

Which was why the Saturday morning in July was such a shock. They were at Sandy's apartment baking bread. Alan was standing in the kitchenette, barefoot and shirtless in his jeans, his arms crossed like some professor looking through round-eyed spectacles at a favorite pupil. Once he had told her jokingly, "Next to making love, the thing I like to do best with you is cook." Sandy, in denim shorts and a Walton State T shirt, was making tiny, graceful kneading motions with her knuckles in the wet dough. "This right?" she asked Alan.

"Come on, lady." He pushed her playfully aside, and a glob of dough dropped onto the floor. "Use some muscle!" Alan threw the entire weight of his body into his hands, vigorously massaging the dough. "Watch how a master chef does it!" She reached into the bag of flour and flung a handful at him, coating his hair and beard. He wheeled around, grabbed some flour and threw it back at Sandy, who squealed and put up her arms to defend herself. "Okay," she called, "truce, truce!" They were both laughing, covered with flour. Alan put the dough in a bowl, placed a towel on top and began wiping himself off. "Now what?" Sandy asked.

"Now it rises," he informed her.

"By itself?"

"Yes," he smiled at her patiently, "all by itself."

"Okay, I'm going down for the mail. And don't be so smart, or I won't even taste the damned bread!"

"Wait a minute," he said, wetting a paper towel. Carefully, like a father scrubbing a little girl's face, he began wiping the flour off her nose, cheeks, and hair. "I don't want the neighbors to talk."

"Gimme that!" She grabbed the towel from him and tried to brush the flour out of Alan's beard. "Ick," she crinkled up her face, "it's sticking."

"Ick yourself." He took the towel out of her hand and kissed her damp nose.

A minute later, as Alan was sponging flour from the counter, he heard the front door open and Sandy cry, "Alan! Alan!" She ran into the kitchen, an open letter fluttering from her hand.

"What is it? What's the matter?" Her face was drained of color, and he saw that her entire body was shaking.

"He's *alive!*" She held the letter out to him, as if this would make him understand. "Roy's *alive!*" She sank down into the dinette chair, clutching the letter to her breast. "My God." She closed her eyes, as if she could not believe it. "My God, he's alive!"

"That's fantastic," Alan said dully, still holding the sponge.

"He's *alive!*" The letter fell from her hands onto the table. She buried her head in her arms. Great, rending sobs tore her body, and she surrendered to them, unable in any way to control her turbulent, conflicting emotions. How could she have thought he was dead? How could she have had so little faith in him? How could she even—

oh, God—have wished him dead, wished him dead, her husband? "I will return to you," said the letter. "Never give up hope." How had this happened to her, this whole crazy nightmare, herself back at school, married but not married, Alan Webber standing shirtless in her kitchen teaching her how to make bread, and in North Vietnam, Roy, her husband, was *alive!*

"Sandy?" She felt Alan's hand lightly on her shoulder and shook it off violently. A memory knifed her, the pleasure she had felt waking up that morning and finding Alan next to her. She covered her eyes with the palms of her hands. My God, she thought, my husband's alive! The enormity of his existence stunned her. I've got to do something, she thought. His parents. They don't even know.

She wiped her eyes and walked over to the kitchen phone. Her legs felt curiously light beneath her. "Who are you going to call?" Alan asked her.

"His folks." She dialed the operator, not looking at Alan. "Operator? I'd like to call Tulsa, Oklahoma, person-to-person, Mrs. Wayne Lawton. The number is 471–4369." She glanced quickly at Alan. "Oh, God, I'm shaking." Alan took a beer from the refrigerator and thought how ironic it was that Sandy should learn of her husband's existence not through the Department of State, the Department of the Air Force, or any of the myriad governmental arms set up to deal with the prisoner problem, but simply from her friendly neighborhood postman.

"Mother Lawton?" she said brightly. "It's Sandy."

"Sandy? Why, how nice to hear from you!" In the trailer park outside Tulsa, Mrs. Lawton was taking bacon out of a frying pan and laying it on a paper towel to drain. "Wayne," she poked her rollered head out the trailer window to her husband, seated in a camp chair reading the *Reader's Digest*. "Wayne, it's Sandy." She was speaking into the phone again. "Sandy, we haven't heard from you lately. We been wondering what you been up to."

"I hope you're sitting down," Sandy said to her mother-in-law, "because I'm going to give you the best news you ever got in your life. Roy is alive!"

"Wayne, she says Roy is alive!" Mrs. Lawton called excitedly out the window. "Wayne!" A gray-haired man in shorts, dark socks, and loafers quickly shuffled into the trailer and stood mutely by the phone. "Sandy, did the Air Force notify you or what?"

"No. I got a letter from him." No reaction from Mrs. Lawton. "Mother, did you hear me? I got a letter from Roy! He's in a prison camp in North Vietnam. He says he's okay, he's feeling okay. Mother?"

Mrs. Lawton ripped off a piece of paper toweling, rubbed the bacon grease off her hands and sat down. "Well, I knew he'd write you first. That's his job, and Roy was always good about that sort of thing."

"Well, I don't think it matters who he wrote first," Sandy said, trying to recover from her astonishment. "I mean, we've heard from him. He's alive!"

"His father and I never doubted that," Mrs. Lawton announced, tight-lipped. Sandy found her mother-in-law's voice particularly nasal and unpleasant through the telephone wires. She remembered the first and only meeting she had had with her in-laws. After Roy had left, they had come to meet her in Florida and taken her to the porpoise show. Ever since then she had always associated her mother-in-law with porpoises, chinless and barking.

Out of the corner of her eye, Sandy saw Alan watering a dying begonia plant. She turned her body toward the telephone, blotting out the sight of him, trying not to pay attention to the fact that he was listening. "Mother," she spoke softly into the phone, "I have prayed to God that Roy was alive. I've prayed daily, but it's been more than two years."

"A mother never gives up," Mrs. Lawton tersely informed her daughter-in-law.

Sandy was beginning to get angry now. "I'm sorry you're upset he wrote me first," she continued, "but I *am* his wife."

"For all of two weeks." In the trailer, Mr. Lawton was making ineffectual gestures to his wife to quiet down, but she turned her back on him and continued. "I gave birth to him, I raised him, I took care of him till the day he joined up," she said. "I've saved every single thing that belonged to him—that's why we're so crowded in this mo-bile home, because I refuse to give up anything that belonged to Roy." She paused only for breath. "You won't understand until you have a son of your own."

Sandy determined to keep her temper. "All right, Mother," she sighed. "I'll be writing to you. Give my regards to Dad." She hung up the receiver.

Across the kitchen, by the window, Alan stood silently staring at her, his hands in the pockets of his jeans. She looked at his vulnerable, questioning face, at the ridiculous white flour on his beard, and she hated him. "Do you mind, Alan," she kept her voice steady with some effort. "I'd really like to be by myself."

He never moved toward her, just looked at her in that same questioning way. "What about us?" he asked softly.

"I don't know." Her voice was sharp. He was an intruder in her apartment, and she wished only for him to disappear and leave her alone to sort out her feelings. "Please go." He reached out toward her as if he wanted to touch her, to say something, but she turned away. For a moment he stood helplessly; then he walked into the bedroom and gathered up his shirt, shoes, toothbrush, and books. He should have known, he thought. He should have known this could happen.

"Will you call me?" He paused by the kitchen door on his way out. But Sandy was rereading Roy's letter, her chin propped in her hands, her mouth curled up ever so slightly, as if at the mention in the letter of some shared memory, Alan thought. He realized she had not even heard his question. Bent over the letter, her hair still messy from bed and from where he had rubbed it with the towel, she looked very beautiful to him. Silently, he let himself out of the apartment.

17

Mrs. Sandra Lawton
2503 Bayline Drive
Tampa, Florida

Dear Mrs. Lawton,

All of us here share your joy at hearing from your husband, Lieutenant Roy D. Lawton, and we greatly appreciate your cooperation in making his correspondence available to us.

May we remind you to handle subsequent letters from your husband with utmost care, with white gloves if possible, and to forward the original of both letter and envelope immediately in the attached glassine envelope.

As you know, letters from prisoners are reviewed by the Department of the Air Force for possible references to other individuals being held captive in the same area. They are also examined by a graphologist, an expert who analyzes handwriting. In keeping with our policy of sharing as much information as possible with the next of kin, we are pleased to summarize for you the graphologist's finding.

The graphologist concludes that Lieutenant Lawton is in a depressed, confused state of mind and suffers from a general lack of alertness. He seems disoriented and withdrawn from reality. This is not unusual, certainly, given the length of his internment.

Mrs. Lawton, may I ask for your cooperation in not discussing this or any other information I have provided regarding prisoner mail outside of your immediate family, and of course under no circumstances should news media be provided with copies of prisoners' letters or results of the graphologist's analysis.

Please do not hesitate to call or write us if you have questions.

Sincerely,
R. V. Claphart, Major, USAF
Directorate of Personnel Services

As soon as she got the letter, Sandy decided she would fly to Washington and visit the graphologist. All she had was one letter from her husband, and it seemed important to any future she tried to construct, to understand as much as possible of Roy's present condition.

Tony Vinza had arranged the meeting through the Department of the Air Force. On a run-down street in northwest Washington, Mr. Desmond Dixon, civilian graphologist, occupied a small, second-floor office which consisted of a desk, two chairs, and an overhead projector mounted on an old typing table. Sandy had the feeling that this room was not for people, only for papers. Mr. Dixon's desk was covered with them, some in piles, some scattered, some piles topped by other piles. Miraculous, she thought, that in that confusion of paper he should have found Roy's letter. But clearly Desmond Dixon had been briefed by the Air Force, because not only had he found Roy's letter, he had already put it next to his 3M projector.

He greeted her quickly. He was a dry, nervous man with a small mustache, shiny black suit, and a high grating voice. "The Pentagon tells me you wish to hear in person my analysis of the alleged letter from your husband." She nodded, though the "alleged" stuck in her mind. "Yes, well, we are used to questions from the layman." He paused briefly, as if this were one of the bur-

dens of any true scientist. "Let me attempt to explain."
He inserted Roy's letter into the projector and flicked on
the light. With a shock, she saw her husband's words to
her blown up across the cracked beige wall of Desmond
Dixon's office and a little black pointer begin to pick at
them as the graphologist spoke.

"Let's take the sentence, 'I love you with all my heart,'"
he began drily. "I assume that's what the writer meant,
that is. There should of course be a 'you' here, between
the 'love' and the 'with.'" The pointer scratched at the
space after the word "love." "This is the sort of thing
that helps us to evaluate your husband's frame of mind."
He paused to pull an inhalator out of his breast pocket
and clear his nostrils. "Excuse me. Now the inability to
complete such a simple sentence would indicate that Lieutenant Lawton is somewhat depressed and withdrawn from
reality. Not unusual, certainly, considering the environment
he has to adjust to in prison camp. One expects a gradual
deterioration." He smiled ever so slightly, almost kindly.
"Now the poor formation of certain of the characters,"
he continued— "the 'y' in 'baby,' the 's' in 'soon'—this
would support my contention that he is less alert than
one would hope."

Sandy determined to keep her composure. "The Air
Force asked me to send along some letters he wrote before
he went down. . . ."

"Yes," Mr. Dixon continued unemotionally, "I used
them for comparison purposes and so I could authenticate
this one as being actually written by your husband."

"Oh, I'm sure it's from Roy."

He smiled patronizingly. "It's understandable that you
would want to think so; it's my job to authenticate it."

"But what I mean is—" Sandy felt flustered, "he used
to leave out words in his other letters, too."

"Not to the same degree." The graphologist was becoming defensive.

"But if you'd check again, I think— You may perhaps have overlooked something?"

"Mrs. Lawton, I'm a little weary of hearing laymen
imply that graphology is an inexact science." By now

Desmond Dixon was definitely testy. "If our results didn't stand the test of time, the military wouldn't be renewing my contract every year." He took several deep breaths to calm himself down and then turned his attention back to the blown-up letter. "Now if there was any doubt of my conclusions," he began, making precise squiggles with the black pointer, "you have only to look at the inconsistent inclination of the letters. Here we are slanting this way, whereas over *here*, we are leaning the other way. . . ."

What the graphologist told her made no sense to Sandy (Roy's letter seemed no different to her from his previous ones), yet she had been brought up to believe in experts, and she felt uneasy. If Roy was in fact confused, withdrawn, and disoriented now, what would he be like by the time he came home?

At the end of the month, she received a routine Air Force information sheet—mimeographed and sent to all primary next of kin. It was entitled "Prisoner Correspondence," and read in part:

Recent experiences with graphological analyses has been far from reassuring. In one case, for example, one of the prisoners was writing fairly regularly, and graphologists were reporting a steady decline in his mental and physical condition. One of the officers released by the North Vietnamese stated that he knew and conversed with the officer, that he was in "great shape," and that his morale was extremely high. Other similar cases have led us to believe that the handwriting may not truly reflect the prisoner's condition.

We have not yet arrived at an explanation for this apparent discrepancy between the graphologists' analyses and the actual state of the men, but we feel we should let you know of this problem. Please be assured we will keep you informed of any further conclusions we may come to about this subject.

LATEST U.S. GOVERNMENT TESTS:
12 MGS. TAR, 0.6 MGS. NICOTINE

TRUE®

Of all leading cigarettes,
True is the only one that puts
its tar and nicotine numbers
right on the front of its pack.

True has nothing to hide.

Latest U.S. Government tests show True is lower in both tar and nicotine than 99% of all other cigarettes sold.

Think about it. Doesn't it all add up to True?

20 CLASS A CIGARETTES

TRUE

FILTER CIGARETTES

LATEST U.S. GOVERNMENT TESTS:
12 MGS. TAR, 0.6 MGS. NICOTINE

Warning: The Surgeon General Has Determined That Cigarette Smoking Is Dangerous to Your Health

She read it once, then reread it and began to laugh.
She remembered what Mary Kaye had been saying with increasing frequency about the military, "Not too many
smarts, you know. . . ."

18

Letter from the Department of the Air Force
to wife after her husband had been interned
for two years:

Dear Mrs. B.,

This is to inform you that your husband,
Technical Sergeant Charles B., has been
selected for promotion to the grade of master
sergeant, United States Air Force.

The announcement of his selection will not
be released to the news media nor will his
name appear on the list of selectees distributed throughout the Air Force. Our
rationale for withholding this information is
to assure that it may not be used to subject
him to any additional pressure or stress.

I share your pride in his selection for
promotion.

"Mommy, what is that stuff?" Julie asked.

"Eye shadow."

"What's it for?"

"To make your eyes look prettier." Sitting at her little
dressing table, Mary Kaye searched through the drawers

for the eye-liner she hadn't used in four years. She was going out on a date with Phil Goratt. He had asked her the other day at school.

"Mommy, are you going on a date with Mr. Goratt?"

"Kathy, will you get your sneakers off my pillow? Of course I'm not going on a date, don't be silly. I already told you, we're going to a teachers' meeting to do some work for the school." In the mirror, Mary Kaye could see the two little girls lolling on her bed, watching her.

Kathy refused to be put off the scent. "Then why are you getting so dressed up?"

"I'm not! Kathy, will you cool it?"

It had been quite casual the way he had asked her. She had spoken to him about the boys, because she simply had to speak to someone. Joe's hostility was so painful for her. Pete worried her too. Lately, he had been unnaturally good, wanting to stay close to her, help her with the housework, tag along with her on errands rather than be with his own friends. Was Pete becoming effeminate? Having no one else to ask, she had spoken to Phil Goratt, the boys' physical education teacher.

"I looked into that situation we were talking about," he'd told her a few days ago in the faculty lunchroom. "Your boys are definitely boys. Nothing wrong in *that* department. But I do think it's time for some heart-to-hearts, especially with Joe. Puberty is just around the corner."

"Phil, I can't!" Mary Kaye was startled.

"It's not that hard, I'll tell you what to say."

"Okay. What *do* I say?"

"Why don't I take you out for a decent meal one of these nights and I'll give you the whole routine?"

Mary Kaye, relieved that he didn't think the boys' problems were serious, realized only several minutes later that he had actually asked her out on a date.

"Mommy?" Julie said.

"Girls, for heaven's sake!"

"I just wanted to tell you you smell good."

Mary Kaye smiled. "Want some?"

Julie and Kathy leaped off the bed and ran to her side.

She showed them how to lift their hair to receive the spray behind their ears. They giggled, sniffing and squealing as the cold spray hit their skin.

"How come you're wearing earrings?" Kathy asked.

"Don't they look all right?" Suddenly insecure, she took one gold hoop off and checked in the mirror again to see which effect was better.

"You're pretty, Mommy. Can I have that dress when I grow up?"

"Absolutely. Only I hope you'll wear it at least two sizes smaller."

The doorbell interrupted the conversation. "Joe?" she called. "Would you answer the door? And try to be civil, please." She replaced the missing earring and quickly transferred her wallet, comb, and handkerchief from the brown leather shoulder-bag to her evening purse. The bell rang again. Joe must have been sitting in front of television purposely refusing to answer the bell for Phil. "Pete? Holy God, will somebody get that doorbell?" She hurried downstairs, the two little girls following close behind.

"I hope you like Italian food," Phil said as he pulled out of the drive. Mary Kaye waved to Julie, who was gazing mournfully out the living-room window. "I made a reservation at Rocco's."

"Fine! I love their food."

"You look very nice," Phil said casually. "I like you in green."

"You look nice yourself. I see you didn't wear your sweat suit."

"I see you didn't wear your brown shoes with the crepe soles." They both laughed.

"Don't say a word about my crepe-soled shoes. They're at least comfortable!"

Phil looked down at her black silk pumps. "I'm glad you opted for discomfort tonight. I love women in high heels."

"Phil, did Monica Corwin reach you? She's collecting for Mr. Nelson's anniversary."

"Back to school business, huh?"

"No, it just occurred to me . . ."

"Yes, I contributed my two dollars and twenty-five cents for the staff gift to our beloved principal. I hear they're getting him a clock-radio. And I still like women in high heels."

Mary Kaye smiled. "Okay, okay. Unaccustomed as I am to going out in public, I find myself short of conversational topics."

"Just relax. You're doing fine."

Rocco's was known as a family-style Italian restaurant, which meant that if a man suddenly decided to treat his family to a weeknight meal, no one had to change clothes. A woman might take her hair out of rollers, but that was about it. Local people flocked here, lured by Rocco's Famous Garlic Toast, the complete dinner price (including hors d'oeuvres and Rocco's Famous Salad), and the homey red-checked tablecloths, topped by unlit candles. Mary Kaye, seated in a booth sipping a drink with Phil, instantly felt overdressed. Around her, kids in polo shirts were valiantly trying to twirl spaghetti around their fork or in some cases simply bending over and shoveling it in with a spoon. Soon, she thought, these people and their children who remind me of my own kids will leave. She remembered her sophomore year in high school when she had greeted her prom date in a tulle formal only to learn that the dance had been switched at the last minute to an outdoor barbecue.

"I think what you gotta talk about," Phil was saying, "is urges. Boys Joe's age begin to have urges— Hell, we all do, even big boys." He smiled at her and she reached for a bread stick, elaborately buttering first one of its narrow sides, then the other. "Also," he continued, "it's always useful to give them some basic nuts and bolts stuff. Physiology. The function of the penis . . . testicles . . . erections. This isn't embarrassing you, is it?"

"God, no!" She gulped the last of her drink. "But could we . . ." She tapped the glass.

"I'm sorry. Miss?" Phil said. The red-haired waitress, her breasts round and high under her shiny black uniform, was taking orders at the next table. "With you in a minute," she said.

Phil turned back to Mary Kaye. "Where were we?"

Mary Kaye cleared her throat. "I guess . . . erections?"

"Right." Phil leaned back in his chair. "Erections." He was wearing a one-button sport jacket and a brown shirt which looked too tight around his neck. Mary Kaye watched him loosen his tie and open the top button of his shirt, revealing a mat of dark hair curling up toward his throat. She looked down at her silverware, rearranging it to make sure the knives and forks were exactly even with the rim of her white plate. "Listen," Phil said, "I got a funny story to tell you. You know Charlie Johnson, the kid with all the freckles? I had him for Hygiene, see, and I'm giving them stuff on the female anatomy, and we're working on Mildred. That's what I call this cutaway model I got, you know, with breasts and a reproductive system. . . ."

"Are you ready to order, sir?" The waitress was at their table, pencil poised over her lined pad.

"Oh, not yet. Bring us another round please. A bourbon and water and a Gibson."

"Say," he turned to Mary Kaye, "could you go for some garlic toast?" Mary Kaye nodded. "Can you bring us an order of garlic toast?" The waitress headed for the swinging doors to the kitchen. "So I was telling you about Charlie. The bell rings, and all the boys get up and go out except Charlie, see. He's sitting there; he's pretending to check some notes he's been making. Finally he gets up and he's holding his books like this, see." Phil took the relish dish from the table and held it over his lap. Mary Kaye laughed and took a bite of her bread stick. "And he starts walking real fast outa the room. I felt so sorry for this poor kid." Phil had a loud laugh. Like everything about him, Mary Kaye thought, it seemed oversized. He popped a large black olive into his mouth as he returned the relish plate to the table. "What you gotta get across to Joe and Pete is that this happens to all boys, this is normal, nothing to be ashamed of. Okay?"

"Okay."

"It's not easy. We all bring our own hang-ups to these things. But ya gotta try for a neutral tone, ya know? Scientific or objective or whatever you want to call it. Ya know," he lowered his voice, suppressing his laughter as he told her this, "one of the gals at the Sex Ed Workshop, she teaches seventh- and eighth-grade girls, she says at night when she's ironing, she practices saying the words out loud—penis, vagina, sexual intercourse," he made ironing motions with his hand, "penis, vagina, sexual intercourse." He laughed and Mary Kaye joined him, though she didn't quite know why she was laughing. Over this last bit of conversation, the waitress had brought their drinks and two large salads, but Phil had continued undeterred, and the waitress smiled, eager to be a good sport. "Say," Phil said, "the salads are real good here. Miss? Don't forget the garlic toast. Ya know,"—he turned back to Mary Kaye, who noted with relief that the family at the next table was leaving; Phil's voice was awfully loud—"some of these kids think hair is going to grow on the palms of their hands, they're gonna go crazy. You know the old wives' tales."

"That's one of the things I most . . . I mean, I don't just say, go right ahead, do I?"

Phil dug his fork into the salad. "They're gonna do it anyway." He chomped at a mouthful of lettuce, romaine and Boston mixed. "Everybody has the same sexual urges. If you don't have an outlet in sexual intercourse, what else are you gonna do?" He speared a cucumber. "How's your salad?"

"Delicious." She picked up her fork and began to eat.

By the time she and Phil had worked their way through large bowls of minestrone and begun on the veal parmigiana, she found herself telling him about her life with Brian. About the endless moves from base to base, about Brian always being away, at the Air Force Academy, in Survival School, on tours of duty, always away. About the kids finally knowing the security of staying put only after their father was in a prison camp. Phil listened attentively.

"You get lonely at times?" he asked.

"Like *all* the time. But you know something? I've discovered a husband is not indispensable. I bought our house myself, I furnished it, I finished my degree, I got a job. We've gotten through three First Communions and four Christmases."

"So what are you saying? You don't need a man?"

"Not in the way you mean. I found out I can live without that, too." Now her voice was soft, barely audible. "But . . . I miss having someone to care for and someone who cares for me."

Phil looked at her. "That's exactly what I miss."

They exchanged a small smile.

After dinner they lingered over brandy-and-sodas. "You know," Mary Kaye said to him, by now a little drunk and teary, "I keep trying to figure out what I did wrong. Brian and I didn't have relations before we were married, we didn't marry out of the faith, we never used anything but the rhythm method. According to the Church, we should be living happily ever after." She smiled at him through her tears, a little ashamed of his seeing her this way, but sensing his sympathy.

"You okay?" He handed her a handkerchief. She nodded. "Hey," he said, "you wanna go over to the Red Rooster? Buddy Sams is still there, I think."

"Sounds great to me." She blew her nose.

> *"You always hurt the one you love*
> *The one you shouldn't hurt at a-all"* *

Buddy Sams, in his maroon Nehru jacket, his light brown toupee tucked tidily over his shiny scalp, held the microphone close to his soft pink lips.

> *"So-o if I broke your heart last night*
> *It's because I love you most of all."* *

The audience applauded, and Buddy bowed graciously. "Thank you, folks, that's one of my favorites, made popular by those wonderful Mills Brothers." He wiped the perspiration from his forehead, leaving a peach-colored streak of make-up on his handkerchief. " 'Course, that was before my time. What's so funny?" He smiled happily at the laughter from the audience. It said to him, everybody loves you, Buddy. "Any requests this evening?"

A gray-haired woman waved her arm. "Buddy?"

"Yes, dear?"

"Are you gonna do Memory Lane tonight?"

"Some of my friends are back tonight, I see. Young lady, I think you were here last night too." He wished it was time for his break so he could go to his dressing room and his bottle of Jack Daniels.

"This is my fourth night in a row," the woman said shyly.

"You come back tomorrow night, too, ya hear?" He winked at her. "I'll be watching for ya."

Buddy dislodged the mike head and with the thick black cord trailing behind him, walked among the tables. At the piano his accompanist sent forth a cover of rippling arpeggios. "Here's how we play Memory Lane," Buddy said. "You call out a year, any year as far back as nineteen twenty, and Rolly and I'll try to remember the song hits of that year. All set, Rolly?"

The accompanist nodded. Buddy stopped at Mary Kaye and Phil's table. "Hi there," he said to Mary Kaye.

"Hi."

"You want to start off tonight? Just name a year, anything back to nineteen twenty." Buddy waited expectantly, but Mary Kaye felt suddenly tongue-tied. "How about the year you two got married?"

Mary Kaye looked quickly down at her drink. Buddy clapped his hand to his mouth. "Uh-oh, ol' Buddy made a boo-boo again!"

A peal of laughter from the audience. Mary Kaye tried to smile, but her cheeks felt taut.

"Buddy," Phil said, "how about nineteen fifty?"

"Nineteen fifty. Nineteen fifty." Buddy started backing

toward the piano area, one hand still circling the microphone, the other pulling the black cord along. "That would be Mr. Nat King Cole and . . .

> *"I want some red roses for a blue lady.*
> *Mr. Florist, take my order please."* *

The audience applauded, then settled back to listen. Mary Kaye looked at Phil, who was watching her with such a worried expression that she had to laugh. He put his arm around the back of her chair pulling it closer to him. She traced the wet circles on the formica table top with her finger.

Later, when Buddy took his break, she and Phil sat chatting quietly.

"Brian and I used to have all these fights about money, did you and Susan?"

"All the time." Phil was playing with the gold bangle on her wrist.

"Yeah, I guess everybody does. But since Bri's been gone, it's sort of pleasant in one way. If I need to get something, I get it. Like if the linoleum needs fixing in the kitchen, you know? I don't have to ask anybody. I just look in my bank balance and if I can afford it, I do it."

"But you're probably very sensible. If I'd let Susan do that, it woulda been over the hill to the poorhouse."

"I betcha Bri would've said the same thing about me." And what would he say if he could see me now, in my green silk dress, with my hair down, a man's arm around my shoulders, so close to me that I can feel his breath on my cheek. "Phil, it's late, we both have to work tomorrow."

"Sure." He signaled for the check.

On the way home in Phil's dark blue Chevy, with a cluster of hockey sticks wedged against the left rear door,

---

* "Red Roses for a Blue Lady" by Sid Tepper and Roy Bennett. Copyright 1948 by Mills Music, Inc. Used by permission.

and a lone volleyball sliding back and forth on the back seat, Mary Kaye settled herself a discreet distance from Phil and pulled her black coat tightly around her.

"I can't afford to get married again, unless Susan remarries, not on what I make," Phil said, lighting another cigarette.

"Do you think she will remarry?"

"Christ, I hope so. Sometimes I think she won't, just for spite." They were entering Silver Grove. The huge billboard was brightly lit. A man and woman holding the hands of a little boy and girl, all four of them standing proudly in front of a split-level home. SEWERS! ALL GAS! CONVENIENT TERMS!

"Also," Phil continued, "how's she gonna meet another guy? She's home all day with the kids." Mary Kaye nodded. She remembered those endless days before the children had started school. She remembered staring out of the window in their small rented house, a prisoner to their colds and ear infections and nap schedules.

"You know something, Mary Kaye? You and I are in the same boat in a funny kind of way, aren't we? Neither of us has a mate, but neither of us can remarry."

"There's the drive, past that white fence there."

Phil swung the car into the drive. The headlights fell for a moment on the scrawny birch tree she and the children had planted in the front yard. "Wrong climate for birches," the nurseryman had told her, but she was determined. "My husband had birch trees in his yard when he was a boy. . . ." They had put it in anyway, but the tree had never really grown. Phil turned off the ignition. She felt very aware of his presence next to her, of his bulk, of the smell of wine and garlic and of Phil.

"I guess I'd better be getting in," she said. He reached over and gently pulled her toward him. She was startled by the roughness of his cheek against her face, by the unaccustomed pleasure of being kissed. She felt an involuntary wetness between her legs and her nipples began to harden. Abruptly, ashamed of her willing body, she pulled away.

"Phil, I'm sorry. I just can't. Please try to understand."

Maybe if things had been different between her and Brian before he left . . .

Phil put his hands back on the steering wheel and drummed his fingers on the plastic rim.

"I'll say goodnight now." Mary Kaye put her hand on the door. "See you tomorrow at school."

"Mary Kaye, you better be careful." His voice sounded cold; or was it merely that he was hurt? "You don't need a man. You're so busy being Wonder Woman, mother, father, and breadwinner all in one, that you aren't going to be good for a goddamned thing when your husband comes home."

His words hit her like stones. She fumbled with the door handle. "I'm sorry," he called to her as she got out, "I didn't really mean that. Mary Kaye?"

Inside the darkened foyer of her house, she leaned heavily against the front door, listening for the sound of his car backing out the driveway. Slowly, still in her coat, she walked through the hall into the living room, turned on the light near the piano bench, and reached deep into the record cabinet, past the children's albums of *The Sound of Music* and *Mary Poppins* and pulled out a worn LP of Jo Stafford songs. She put it on the record player and sat down on the couch to listen to "You Belong to Me."

Within minutes, Julie straggled sleepily downstairs, her braids flopping against her light blue nightgown. Mary Kaye patted the couch, and Julie snuggled next to her. Mary Kaye rested her cheek on the little girl's hair, and together they listened to the music.

19

Letter from the Department of the Air Force

Dear Air Force Next of Kin,

This is to advise you as well as the next of kin of all other captured personnel in North Vietnam of a new development regarding American prisoners of war in that country.

Based on information derived from recent Communist news releases, our government feels that increased pressure is quite possibly being brought to bear on our personnel being held captive by the North Vietnamese in an attempt to force them to make unfavorable statements against their country. These statements would be given world-wide publicity for the purpose of trying to degrade and sway world opinion against the efforts of the United States in Southeast Asia. As you may remember, the exact same thing was done by the Communists during the Korean War, some sixteen years ago.

I am truly sorry that the contents of this letter could not be of a happier nature; how-

147

> ever, I felt certain that you would want to
> be apprised of anything that could possibly
> affect your husband.

The first national meeting of the Association of POW/ MIA Relatives was held in Chicago in the spring of 1970. Though it was hardly a gala event, dealing as it did with an unhappy subject and held in the shabby ballroom of one of Chicago's least elegant hotels, the meeting attracted over eight hundred people, seeking not elegance but a variety of goals more important to them: publicity for a cause, a chance to influence Association policy, a forum to air their questions, or simply the comfort of numbers. Roberta Penny, chairman of the Association and wife of an MIA, was pleased at the turnout. All branches of the services were represented, she noted, watching the families enter the cavernous room and take their seats. The subject of the address was one she knew to be of intense interest to the families since they themselves had selected it from three possible topics on a questionnaire mailed out earlier. "What Will He Be Like When He Returns?" was the provocative theme of their guest speaker, Major Bernard Rosen, an Army psychologist, and it had won handily over "The Benefits and Disadvantages of Direct Protest Action" and "Mail Routes—Which One Is Best?"

For the women in the audience, the national meeting was also a chance to catch up on news, see military families they had known from previous bases, and chat with the brass who had been invited to attend. Toward the back of the room, Margaret Holroyd, Sandy, and Mary Kaye were seated together. "Hey, I've got something juicy," Margaret reported. "Remember that gal from Milwaukee, Sally Scofield?"

"Yeah, where is she?" Mary Kaye asked. "I haven't seen her. She always comes to everything."

Margaret shook her head smugly. "No more."

"Come on, give!" Mary Kaye sat forward with curiosity.

"She remarried."

"What!"

"Yup," Margaret said, proud of the scoop, "she went to court and said he's been missing for three years and to the best of her knowledge, he's dead."

"And they let her? Jesus, what if he shows up one of these days?" Mary Kaye shook her head.

Sharon Dornbeck was seated next to her mother, her navy bag placed on the empty chair next to her. Reserved for Daddy, Sandy thought to herself. She waved to Sharon and received a cold smile in return. "Hey, I didn't tell you," Sandy turned to Mary Kaye, "I got another letter from Roy just before I left."

"Good!"

"It's just like the last one only it's forty-two words instead of forty-one."

"Well, that's progress," Mary Kaye said with acerbity.

"I mean, I'm glad to get it and all, but it doesn't say anything." She hesitated. "It's sort of a letdown, know what I mean?"

"Wait till you have nineteen of them like I do." Mary Kaye smiled. "Sandy," she lowered her voice, "what are you going to do about Alan?"

"Mary Kaye! How can I see him now that I know Roy is alive? I just can't!"

"Groovy! Now you can miss both, Roy *and* Alan!"

No, Sandy thought, just Alan. "Well, you're one to talk—true blue for four and a half years!"

"Yeah, but I'm in a different situation. Think of the logistics problems I've got. Joe baby-sits for me when I go out, right? I have to leave him a phone number where I'll be in case of emergency. So what would I do, say, 'Joe dear, I'll be down at the Holiday Inn Motel. If someone gets sick, just call me and I'll jump into my clothes and be home in ten minutes'?"

Sandy laughed. "Anyway, Alan's stopped calling by now. He's gotten the message." She thought fleetingly of their last bitter phone conversation, while she nodded to Mrs. Kubichek and Mrs. Calafano, who had come in together. Better not to think of Alan. The hall was almost full now, and the meeting should begin soon.

In an anteroom off the main ballroom Jerry Gundersen was talking with his old buddy General Fletcher Gibbs, USAF, whom he hadn't seen since Korea. He had been hoping for some inside information about his son-in-law; instead he found himself, not unwillingly, on the receiving end of one of Gibby's famous nonstop perorations.

"Jerry," Gibby was saying, running a comb needlessly through his gray crew cut, "I got wives coming in and begging me to change their guys from missing in action to killed in action so they can remarry. I got one wife from California, she says I don't want to hear from you people. Guy's been in a POW camp *six* years. She says don't write me or call me unless he's coming home or he's dead." Gibby put the comb away in his breast pocket. "I got a mother from Texas, calls me once a week like clockwork to tell me her son's wife is shacking up with another guy, so *she* wants to be declared primary next of kin. Jesus," he paused briefly, "this job's worse than combat in 'Nam!" Jerry chuckled sympathetically. "I got one wife, husband was killed in action, she refuses to believe it; she's sure he's alive and in a POW camp. I need a two-martini lunch most days or I can't get through the afternoon!"

In the main ballroom Roberta Penny decided that it was time to begin. She stepped to the dais and welcomed the group. "I want to read you all a telegram which we just received from Senator O'Keefe. 'Our accomplishments on behalf of the missing and captured have been modest, but don't be discouraged. Right now we have more momentum going for us than ever before. The latest resolution by the joint session of Congress cannot help but register on the minds of the enemy that the Congress of the United States cares.'"

The burst of laughter from the audience surprised Roberta Penny and annoyed General Fletcher Gibbs, as he made clear when he spoke later.

"Well, I'm just plain amazed at you people!" Gibby thundered, clutching the microphone in his best give-'em-hell expression. "We're doing the best we by God can, you can just bet your boots we are! And anybody who doesn't think so can say it to my face. I'd like one of you to say right to my face, Gibby, you aren't trying hard enough. Because we are out there twenty-four hours a day, three hundred sixty-five days a year, workin' our tails off for our boys. And we aren't about to stop!" The audience was responding now, its cynicism soothed by the glitter of military medals and by the honest conviction of Fletcher Gibbs himself. Gibby lowered his voice. "Just remember, don't let yourselves become the stereotyped version of what people think women are!"

Sandy turned quizzically to Mary Kaye. "He means bitches," Mary Kaye explained.

Gibby was in high gear now, winding up for the finish, his fists moving toward the audience, punching home his points. "Hang in there. The enemy is hurting and we aren't gonna let up! No, sir! We aren't gonna let up—so don't you either!" The audience was won over, the applause thunderous. Sharon, Jerry and Paula Gundersen and a handful of others rose to their feet. "Ol' Gibby, he's battin' a hundred per cent!" Jerry said, applauding enthusiastically, and Sharon and her mother nodded, gazing in admiration at the general.

Major Bernard Rosen's manner was in direct contrast to General Fletcher Gibbs's. A slow and careful man, he spoke precisely, putting on tortoise-shell glasses to consult notes occasionally, meticulously choosing his words. "I am happy to address you today," Major Rosen began, "on the subject of what you may anticipate on that long-awaited day, when your loved one returns." Sandy didn't know whether it was Major Rosen's lugubrious manner or his choice of the phrase "loved one" that reminded her of an undertaker. "Let me say right at the outset that whatever you have gone through so far, when your loved one returns, you will have to grapple with a whole new set of problems. Do I make myself clear?" Major Rosen was also a master of the rhetorical question, trained to look directly at his audience to make sure he was *communicating*. "Your problems are not over when your loved one returns; indeed," he paused here for emphasis, "they are really just beginning." A silence settled over the room. "During your loved one's imprisonment, he was withdrawn and apathetic. But behind that apathy lay another feeling. Anger. When he comes home, he is going to exhibit that anger to you who love him. You must therefore be prepared for hos-tile reactions." Major Rosen broke the word "hostile" into two sharp syllables, hissing the "s." "Now," he continued, "how should you handle these hos-tile reactions?" There was not a sound in the hall. "Help him to talk about his anger. Listen. Don't be tempted when he tells you how bad it was for him, to say, 'Well, but let me tell you how bad it was for *me!*' Your job is to listen and help him with what is bothering him."

Sandy tried to imagine Roy hostile and angry. She had never known him that way. They hadn't even been married long enough to have a fight. Roberta Penny was at the microphone now, opening the floor to questions. She called on a young wife whom Sandy did not know.

"Is it likely that the men will have sexual problems when they return?" the girl asked.

"Good question," the psychologist commented—he was trained to put people at their ease—"because it expresses what everyone wants to know but most are afraid to ask, to paraphrase the title of a book many of us have been reading." General laughter. "Yes," he continued, picking his words even more carefully than usual, "sexual problems are not uncommon in returning prisoners. The literature dealing with imprisoned people is quite clear on this point. Now, what form will this difficulty take? Problems of impotency have been well noted, and, of course"—he paused here—"we do not know what exposure the prisoner may have had to homosexual contact." Mrs. Calafano crossed herself, and Sharon Dornbeck whispered, "This is disgusting." Her mother nodded. "Certainly," Major Rosen continued, "the men will be depressed, and people who are depressed are less interested in sex." He paused, and perhaps sensing how deeply disturbing his words were, added, "The odds are good, however, that in time the depression will vanish and with it those difficulties." He smiled. "As I look around, I expect the men will soon be quite stimulated." Sandy joined in the general laughter, though she in no way felt mirthful.

Roberta Penny was pointing to Mary Kaye, whose arm was raised. "Mary Kaye Buell, I knew you'd have a question."

"I have dozens," Mary Kaye said, standing up, "but I'll confine myself to this one. We aren't going to have a military victory. And while some Americans think our husbands are heroes, others think they are anything from war criminals to just plain suckers. Now, Major Rosen, how can we help our men deal with that?"

The major looked somewhat uncomfortable. "I am not equipped to handle political questions," he began. "However, you have put your finger on an important point that I think all of you should be aware of. When he returns, your loved one may have severe guilt feelings. Why guilt feelings? Not because he questions the war, but simply because he was captured. Even if that capture was not his fault, he may feel that it was. He may feel that he sinned by allowing himself to be taken in the first place."

Sandy's head was beginning to pound. She had been able to dismiss the graphologist's report because the Air Force itself admitted that graphological analyses were not always correct, but the word of a psychologist, a trained scientist, was different. Despite the fact that she didn't particularly like Major Rosen, she believed him. The shaky future she had been trying, with considerable effort, to construct for Roy and herself began to crumble. After Major Rosen's speech, she could not picture the return of the cocky, fun-loving boy she had married. What the psychologist described was a sexually incompetent, guilt-ridden invalid. At the age of twenty-one, having spent more than two years of her life waiting for his return, she was now supposed to play the understanding nursemaid. It was all right for the POWs to feel anger, Major Rosen had said; everyone was expected to be sympathetic. Hell, what about *her* anger? What about *her* life?

She filed out of the hotel's gala ballroom with Margaret and Mary Kaye. In the parking lot, General Gibbs's heli-

copter was perched in ungainly readiness. With a jaunty
wave and a hearty smile to the women, he climbed into
the waiting chopper, and lifted off out of their lives as
casually as he had dropped in. "Come on, San," Mary
Kaye said, heading toward the bus, "*our* Cobra awaits."

"No, thanks, Mary Kaye, I think I'll take a taxi back to
the hotel, then head on back home right away."

Mary Kaye looked at her, surprised. "You mean you're
gonna miss the raunchy wives' dinner?"

"Yup, that's one dinner I think I'll miss." Mary Kaye
was still looking at her with concern as Sandy hailed a
passing cab.

It was past midnight when she arrived at Alan's, but
he was still up studying. When he opened the door, he
looked exactly the way she remembered him, rumpled and
very dear. In the background the stereo was on.

"Bach?" she asked softly.

"Handel," he said.

"Oh." She was still holding her suitcase.

"You never were too good at music," he said, looking
down at her tenderly and reaching for her suitcase.

The next day she moved in.

20

From Newsletter of National League of Families of American Prisoners and Missing in Southeast Asia

Among the many projects being undertaken by individuals or groups on behalf of the Prisoners and Missing is the "POW/MIA Bracelet" being distributed by VIVA. Because Bob Hope is honorary Chairman of this project and many Hollywood stars are involved, there will undoubtedly be a great deal of publicity on this effort. . . .

"Mrs. Dornbeck?"

"Yes."

"This is Ed Baldwin talking. That name ring any bells?"

"No, I'm afraid not."

"Oh, I thought maybe your husband had written to you about me. We flew in the same squadron."

"You flew in Richard's squadron?" Sharon grabbed the phone more tightly.

"Yes, ma'am, I did, and since I was passing through Tampa, I thought I just couldn't leave without dropping by to see you. I just got back from Vietnam myself a few weeks ago."

"Oh, please, Ed, you come on right over!" Sharon gave

him the address and quickly ran upstairs, showered, and put on a freshly ironed crisp cotton dress. She combed her hair carefully and dabbed perfume behind her ears. Someone who had seen Richard was coming, someone who could tell her what he was like over in Vietnam— what he talked about, thought about. "Ricky," she called, "you come put on a clean shirt. We're gonna meet a man who flew airplanes with Daddy." Her parents were out, so she changed the child's outfit herself and then checked in the refrigerator to make sure there was enough iced tea.

Ed Baldwin was blond and clean-cut looking, with the kind of open, warm good looks that Richard had. In fact, she thought, he looked like a smaller, slighter version of her husband. "Hope I'm not interrupting anything," he smiled at her.

"Oh no, I'm so glad you came! Ricky, this is Lieutenant Baldwin. Shake hands." Ricky solemnly extended his hand and Ed shook it formally. Sharon smiled. "Now why don't you go outside and play, darlin'?" Ricky ran out the door and Sharon showed Ed into the living room. "You want some iced tea?"

"Thanks." He sat down in Jerry Gundersen's favorite chintz armchair. "I just figured as long as I'm here, I couldn't go away without paying my respects to Captain Dornbeck's wife."

Sharon poured two glasses of iced tea, handed one to Ed, and sat down. "You were in Richard's squadron?" she said, trying to draw him into talking about her husband.

"Yes, I sure was." He took a long sip of his iced tea and placed the glass carefully on a coaster. "I just want to tell you the guys were all crazy about him. Captain Dornbeck was just . . . just, well, somethin' special." He shook his head, unable to express his feelings.

"I know," Sharon smiled. "I feel just the same way about him myself."

"He showed me your picture once," Ed said.

"He did?"

"You and your little boy." He glanced through the living-room window at Ricky climbing on the jungle gym.

"Yup," he shook his head, "they say the good ones always get it, and it's true."

"Want some spice cake?" Sharon offered. Ed shook his head. "Where are you headin' now, Ed?"

"Back to North Dakota. I'm from Ohio myself, but my girl, she's from Minot. I met her when I was stationed there before I went over, and I'm real anxious to see her."

"I'll bet you are!"

"Yeah, well," Ed looked down at the carpet, then up at Sharon. "I don't want to take up any more of your time. I just came by, like I said, to pay my respects and tell you how sorry the guys are about Captain Dornbeck. Good as he was, nobody coulda made it outa that bird alive." Sharon straightened up, looking at him in amazement, but he continued right on. "If it'd just been the tail, he mighta' had a chance. He was flyin' low bird— Jesus, he took a direct hit right in the belly of the plane."

"What are you sayin'?" Sharon sat forward, putting her drink down. "My husband got out!"

Ed shook his head politely. "It's possible, but I don't think so."

"My husband's missin'!" Sharon insisted. "They heard his beeper twice."

"Mrs. Dornbeck, I was there. You have to understand, we had a triple canopy of jungle underneath. Even if he did eject . . ."

"Lieutenant," Sharon stood up, "I'll thank you to leave my home. And don't ever come back!" She walked to the front door and held it smartly open for him.

"Mrs. Dornbeck . . ." Ed stood by the door, twisting his Air Force cap in his hands.

"Not another word! I won't listen!"

"I'm sorry," Ed mumbled as he left.

Sharon shut the door behind him and sat back down again, her hands shaking as she picked up her iced tea.

21

Letter from the Department of the Air Force

Dear Air Force Next of Kin,

As you know, the Air Force has formulated a plan which provides for the expeditious processing of repatriated prisoners of war. In conjunction with this plan, information brochures and next-of-kin photographs, which will be given to the returnees, are currently on file in Southeast Asia. . . .

This brings to light a problem. Some next of kin have passed away subsequent to the time certain of our missing-in-action and captured members were downed over enemy territory. . . .

Realizing that the first concern of a returnee will be his family, and knowing that he will have many immediate questions about their welfare, it will be extremely difficult to withhold information about the death of a close relative for any period of time. Therefore, we believe it may be in the best interests of the returnee to be apprised of this information without delay, provided that the attending physician agrees to such a notification. . . .

It would be appreciated if those of you who
have previously advised us of a death in the
immediate family, but who have not apprised
us of the cause and date, provide this information to us. . . . A self-addressed envelope
is attached for your use in the event our
files indicate that our information is in-
complete. . . .

Whereas Sandy's two-week marriage to Roy had been
more like an affair, her affair with Alan was more like a
marriage. She knew him better than her husband, knew
that he liked garlic in his hamburger, was grumpy in the
morning, had little tolerance for her country rock music
(though he liked to watch her move to it), became
nervous whenever he called his parents, wore only Levis
or wash pants himself but loved to see Sandy in dresses.
She knew too that he needed her, not romantically as Roy
had, or even merely sexually, but in a deeper sense, to
give himself confidence, to build his own sense of worth.
He made a religion of self-deprecation, and it was her
role to tear down the pagan idols. "Big deal, teaching
education at a second-rate state college," he would say,
and she would encourage him, telling him that it was
worthwhile to go on and finish his Ph.D.—because Sandy
truly believed it was. She did not think him second-rate in
any sense, and before her he could not consider himself a
failure either. It was a powerful lure.

She was eminently moldable, and quite willing to be
reshaped according to Alan Webber's vision. Having abandoned most of the trappings of her old life—it seemed ages
ago to her that she had been a teller in a bank—she was
searching for a new one. A girl who would have been a
traditional housewife and mother, except for an accident
over the skies of North Vietnam, had become liberated in
spite of herself. She was reading Alan's books now, Fanon
and Cleaver, Reich and Betty Friedan, and though she
did not understand them completely, they had changed her

enough so that she knew she could never unquestioningly resume her former life.

Her sexual habits had changed too. Though she had been aroused by Roy's passionate need for her— "I'll never get enough of you," he had said— yet each time they finished and Roy slumped over her with momentary exhaustion, she had felt unresolved, unfinished. Patiently she waited for her moment of release, but it never came. "Did'ja like it, Sandy?" he always said. "Oh, sure!"

Alan didn't wait around for any miracles. "Does this feel good?" he would ask. "How about this?" With his fingers and his tongue he knew how to bring her body to such a pitch—her stomach and inner thighs prickling with desire, her nipples hardened—that by the time he penetrated her, she felt a wild urgency. There was no faking things with Alan, but there was no need to. He liked variety. "What's so sacred about man over, woman under?" he would tease her. "I just always thought that's how it's supposed to be." "There's no 'supposed to be.'" He showed her a paperback with illustrations of one hundred positions and told her his ambition was to invent at least ten new ones. He liked to put hard rock on the stereo—it was the only time he strayed from classical music—and time their sex to climactic musical moments. Sometimes he would read aloud to her from porno books that were making the campus rounds. And always, he seemed to take as much pleasure from her response as from his own.

Yet she was unwilling to abandon completely her old life. She kept her apartment, partly out of convention (what would she tell her parents, Roy's folks, the Air Force? The address would have to say c/o Webber), and partly out of the sense that she was still married to Roy. She felt a sweet sad fondness for him, although as the months wore on, he seemed more and more like a dear and distant friend to whom she still felt some residual obligation. She wrote him cheerful, forced letters, and every few months she would hear from him in return. He seemed to have as little impact on her life as Dennis, her old high-school boyfriend.

Except for Mary Kaye, she hardly saw the wives from the Tampa group any more, which was why she was surprised to hear from Diane Devere. She had stopped by her apartment to pick up the mail when the phone rang. "Sandy? My God, where *have* you been? I've been trying you for days!" Diane went on to explain that she was to be the featured speaker at the Forum, Walton State's weekly discussion meeting. "Sandy, I'm so nervous. The only reason I said yes is because Margaret said you go to Walton. You've got to come and hold my hand."

"Okay, relax. I'll be there. In fact, I'll take you out for a cup of coffee first."

"Better make it after. I sincerely believe I will throw up anything I eat beforehand!"

Sandy and Alan met Diane beforehand and walked her around the campus, pointing out the Boat Pond and what Alan called "other points of disinterest."

Diane's hair was sprayed into a high bouffant globe, thick green eye shadow plastered on her eyelids. She and Sandy were the same age, yet she seemed like a visitor from another world. My Lord, Sandy thought, *I* used to dress like that, *I* used to look like that.

Later that evening, Diane was nervous as she took the stage. "I am not a political person," she began softly, her eyes ranging across the casually attired students in the Marshall Auditorium, "but I feel that the issue of POWs and MIAs transcends whatever political differences we may have. I have come here tonight to urge you to rally behind our efforts to force Hanoi to stop its inhuman treatment of the prisoners and to release the names of all captured men." When she spoke briefly of her husband, her son, and her seven-month-old baby, whom Jim had never seen, several of the girls in the audience looked at her with sympathy. But later, she began defending the administration, and Sandy looked down at the floor, knowing that Diane was a lamb prancing toward the sacrificial altar, the students the high priests sharpening their knives. They'll do her in in the question period, Sandy thought. She tucked her hand inside Alan's and gripped his fingers tightly.

The first question came from a tall, thin boy with a peace symbol emblazoned on his sweat shirt. "Your husband is a career officer, isn't he?" "Yes," Diane replied, "he's career, but he's not an officer, he's enlisted."

"You military people make a big deal over that officer/enlisted stuff, don't you?"

"Is that your question?" Diane asked nervously and seemed surprised when the room rang with laughter.

"My question is this," retorted the boy, reddening. "Your husband chose to go. That's his career. I hope you get him back, but frankly, what really counts is ending the war. That's what we ought to rally behind!" A claque of students cheered, and the boy looked around triumphantly.

"May I answer your question, if there was one? Yes, my husband chose to go and at least he had the joy of living by his principles." She looked at the boy defensively. "From that peace symbol on your shirt, I guess you believe in the peace movement?" He nodded proudly. "And yet *you* choose to sit around on a college campus instead of devoting yourself full time to what *you* believe in!"

Once again the audience cheered. The boy sat down abruptly. "I never knew she had it in her," Sandy whispered to Alan.

The next question came from a girl in a paisley-printed granny dress. Her long fine hair fell along the sides of her face giving her the appearance of a rabbit peeping out of a hutch. "I just want to say it's real sad about your baby and all, but when are you POW wives gonna cotton up to the fact that you're just pawns for the administration?"

Here we go, Sandy thought. "Indeed we are," Diane said angrily. "We're also pawns of the peace movement." There were some hisses from the audience, and a faint pink crossed Diane's usually sallow cheeks. The questions grew increasingly hostile, and Diane became more and more flustered. Alan slipped out of the row and hurried down the aisle to whisper to the faculty adviser, Dr. Henderson. Within a few minutes, Henderson adjourned the meeting.

"Why did you do that, Alan?" Sandy asked when he

came back. He shrugged. "She said what she came to say. They were tearing her apart." He rested his forearms on her shoulders and leaned his face close to hers. "And I figured that would make you very unhappy."

Later Sandy and Diane went out for coffee. "Sandy, do you mind if I say something?" Diane stirred her coffee idly. "I like Alan, he seems very nice—I was a little afraid of him at first, him being a professor, but he's easy to talk to and he's real nice." She paused.

"Go ahead," Sandy said.

"But you don't belong with these kids."

"Where *do* I belong?"

Diane frowned. "What are you talking about? Have you given up on Roy? Is that it?"

Sandy shook her head. "It doesn't have anything to do with Roy. I'm in love with Alan, Diane, and I guess I belong wherever he is."

Diane's remarks continued to reverberate in Sandy's mind long after her visit to the campus. For the next several weeks, although her feelings for Alan were more complex and compelling, Roy was on her mind. She didn't even know if she'd entirely stopped loving him. In his last letter he had written, "I still love the girl I married," as though he had a premonition that that girl no longer existed.

One night, when she and Alan had finished making love and were lying quietly, their arms around each other, Sandy sat up suddenly, pulling the sheet modestly around her, and turned to face Alan. "I want you to tell me something." She looked at him quizzically. "Have I changed a lot since you've known me?"

He lay on his side, one arm stretched out under his head. His fluffy brown hair made an even halo on the pillow. Sandy had been trimming it just before, moving in a slow intimate dance around him. Wisps of Alan's hair still lay on the floor and now on the pillow. "Why?" he asked.

"Just tell me your honest opinion."

"Well," he teased, tracing the outline of her thigh

through the sheet, "you've learned how to bake bread. . . ."

"Come on," she pleaded, springing backward on the bed, out of his reach, "I'm serious."

"What is it?" Alan asked, turning away from her. "Roy again?"

Sandy sat hugging her knees, immersed in her own thoughts. "Sometimes I think if he came home, he'd take one look at me and run the other way. I mean, he'll have changed, too, but— Oh, God, I don't know."

"You know," Alan said angrily, "this is getting to be a habit with you. The minute we're finished in the sack you start talking about Roy."

"I do not!" Sandy protested, immediately realizing he was right, sensing how she had hurt him.

"Yes, you do. Who were you making love to just now, me or him?"

Wordlessly, Sandy slid down into his arms and began stroking his face, trying to tell him through her touch that he was right, that she was sorry. Later when he made love to her again, he was wild, savage, wanting to hurt her, make her cry. It frightened her. Afterward, she looked at him differently, sensing that their relationship had passed into a new stage. She felt her body bore the imprint of his love, and she realized that whatever happened from now on, their lives were irrevocably intertwined.

But that realization came shortly before their affair ended.

22

Letter from the Department of the Air Force

Dear Air Force Next of Kin,

Postmaster Winton M. Blount recently announced that two postage stamps on military themes will be issued later this year. One honors today's US servicemen, particularly those who are prisoners of war or missing or killed in action. The second marks the 50th anniversary of the Disabled American Veterans, a service organization that has aided more than 1.5 million disabled veterans and their families. Both 6-cent stamps will be printed on the same sheet. The date and place of issuance will be announced later. . . .

Mr. Blount stated: "By issuing these two stamps, we pay homage to all American servicemen living and dead. But we have special interest in those who today endure a form of living death, imprisoned by the North Vietnamese and the Viet Cong, the fate of many remaining unknown to their families. Millions will know by the appearance of these stamps that this nation urges an immediate

and unconditional release of all prisoners of
war held by both sides in Indochina. As
President Nixon has said, it is time that war
and imprisonment ends for all these
prisoners. They and their families have
already suffered too much."

Seated at the center of the head table of the Rotary Club,
Sharon scraped the mushroom sauce off her chicken breast
and pushed it to the side of the plate along with the po-
tatoes *au gratin*. Next she did the same for the dollop of
mayonnaise topping a red, fruit-filled gelatin square.

"Don't tell me *you* have to count calories," Red Fortner said, waving a freckled hand in the air to signal the
waiter.

Sharon smiled. She spoke in a low, confidential tone
which caused Red to lean closer for her words. "Now,
Mr. Fortner, you weren't supposed to notice. You
peeked." There was something in her tone which made
Red feel very good indeed. He was old enough to be her
father, and yet she had a flirtatious quality which he
found invigorating.

"Mr. Wallingford," Sharon turned to the man on her
right, "I want to thank you gentlemen for this lovely cor-
sage. I don't think anyone has sent me gardenias since
high school."

"Is that so?" Charlie Wallingford beamed. "I had
quite a little discussion with the florist on that score, I
don't mind telling you. We aren't fortunate enough to have
beautiful young lady guest speakers very often." The sun,
gleaming in through the high windows of the private hotel
dining room, glinted off the tiny American flag pinned to
Sharon's collar and made her squint slightly. Charlie Wallingford, ever attentive to his responsibilities as Program
Chairman, asked if the light was bothering her.

"You're mighty kind, but I'm a real Florida baby. I
love the sunshine. Mr. Wallingford, won't you tell me
just a little bit about the activities of your chapter here?"
She inserted a bite of chicken into her mouth, careful not

to blur her lipstick, and fixed her thick-lashed blue eyes on Charlie Wallingford's plump pink face. When she had first overcome her shyness and begun speaking to civic groups, she had discovered that the Charlie Wallingfords of the world were just like the boys she dated at college. If you looked at them hard, laughed at their jokes, and asked them questions about themselves, they carried the conversational ball for minutes at a time.

This morning, as Ricky watched her put on her make-up and dress to go, he had asked, "Do you have to go out *again?*" "Yes," she had answered sharply. Lately she had been feeling edgy. The sleeplessness she had experienced before going to Paris had returned, and this time, for no particular reason, she felt nervous at the thought of speaking before a group, though she had been giving the same speech for months now, poised and confident to the outside world.

"Once a year my wife and I go deep-sea fishing," Charlie Wallingford was saying. "Greatest sport in the world."

"Oh, really? What kind of fish do you catch, Mr. Wallingford?" She'd make it up to Ricky later, when Richard came home. She put down her fork; the chicken was tasteless.

If Richard came home . . .

The lectern at which she was to give her speech rested on the white cloth in the center of the table. Red Fortner hurried over to remove the large spray of orange and yellow flowers so that none of his fellow Rotarians would suffer an obscured view of her. Some of the men were lighting cigars, others pulling their chairs around so they wouldn't have to crane their necks. While Charlie Wallingford placed a pitcher of ice water and a glass near the lectern, Sharon looked down the long table, which formed a T with the speaker's table, and wondered why she was feeling so nervous. In her desk at home there were twenty-three thank-you notes, all written by program chairmen like Charlie Wallingford, from Rotary Clubs, Kiwanis Clubs, church groups, American Legion Posts, and VFW chapters as far south as Miami and as far west as Mobile. The waiters had now finished whisking away the strawberry parfaits and coffee; the room was quiet. Sharon stood at the lectern and began speaking.

"My husband is Captain Richard Dornbeck of the United States Air Force." Her voice lilted upward at the end of each phrase. "And I would like to tell you what happened to him. Because what happened to Richard has happened to thousands of our countrymen." The Rotarians listened intently. Cigars went out unnoticed. Several of the men who had planned to leave early for afternoon business appointments forgot about the time. What *did* happen to Richard, Sharon wondered suddenly and pushed the thought away. "My husband was hit by enemy fire over Haiphong. The emergency beeper of his plane sounded twice, and then the plane went down. He is listed by our government as Missing in Action." The face of Ed Baldwin saying, "Nobody coulda made it outa that bird alive" intruded before her eyes.

"Last year I went to Paris to try to find out if I was a wife or widow." She gripped the edge of the lectern and told them of the failure of her trip and of the films she had been shown. Then she talked about Ricky.

"I have a little boy who still looks up when a jet plane goes by and says, 'Is that my daddy?' My son came home from his first day at school cryin' his heart out because all the other little boys had daddies and he didn't."

Red Fortner felt an unaccustomed clutch in his throat. Those savages over there! We ought to bomb the hell out of them, blast them from the face of the earth! He wished some of his dove colleagues at the office could hear this girl, so young, so pretty, so brave, without even a father for her child! They'd change their tune all right. He decided to go up afterward and invite her to address the Men's Club at the First Presbyterian next month. That's the kind of girl young Bob should bring home for a change, instead of those abominations with their frizzy hair and their pink-o ideas.

"What can you do to help?" Sharon was asking the silent room. "You can join me in starting an avalanche of letters to Hanoi, demanding that the North Vietnamese comply with the Geneva Convention on humane treatment of prisoners. You can join me in wiring your congressmen and the President, declaring your support of the administration's efforts to obtain the prisoners' release." The men applauded these suggestions, and Sharon's closing remarks brought them to their feet. "In my heart," she said, and she had the sudden eerie sensation that she was outside herself, listening to her own voice critically, skeptically, "I have faith that my husband is still alive. He and all our missing men will someday be safe at home again, with God's help—and yours!"

Afterward, many of the Rotarians surged up to the speaker's table to thank Sharon for her speech. She shook hand after hand, demurring gracefully at the praise, listening for and repeating each of the men's names. The heavy odor of the gardenias pinned to her dress seemed like an intoxicant.

"Mrs. Dornbeck, I'm Jack Frank." The man had unnaturally bushy eyebrows that met in a straight line over his dark, intent eyes.

"I'm happy to meet you, Mr. Frank."

"I want to tell you you're just about the bravest little girl I ever laid eyes on." His look was worshipful, like a religious fanatic eyeing a venerable object; it made her uncomfortable.

"You're very kind, Mr. Frank, but I'm not really."

"Yes, ma'am, you are. I sat there listening to you, and it made me sick!"

Sharon's forehead wrinkled involuntarily. Had she heard him correctly?

"Us sitting here looking at that beautiful face of yours, and your husband would probably give anything in the world to see you right this minute. Made me sick to my stomach!"

Jack Frank stared at her intently, as if by the holy passion of his look he could keep her inviolate. With relief, Sharon saw that Charlie Wallingford was coming to steer her past these dangerous shoals like the jolly little tugboat in the story she often read to Ricky.

"Mrs. Dornbeck?" Charlie bubbled. "Can I tear you away?" He put his arm around her shoulder with a proprietary air. "There's some folks want to take your picture."

In no more than a second, Jack Frank yanked Charlie's arm from her shoulder and violently punched Charlie in the mouth. "Don't you touch her!" Frank shouted. "You have no right to lay a hand on this little girl!"

For a moment, his fellow Rotarians seemed stunned by Jack Frank's bizarre outburst. Then, several of them restrained him, while others tended to Charlie. Suddenly, as she watched, Sharon began to giggle. Not with amusement, but with a bizarre, uncontrollable sound utterly divorced from the slim body and Revlon-tinted lips through which it forced its way. They were all looking at her now, even Charlie with his bloody lip, but she couldn't stop herself. She pressed her hand against her mouth as though to push the inappropriate sound back inside, but it popped out with even greater intensity, like an uncoiling jack-in-the-box. It was all ridiculous, them fighting over her, her being here, everything she was saying.

Suddenly Sharon was sobbing, great heaving gasps which ricocheted painfully across her chest. "He's dead!" she screamed at the cluster of startled Rotarians. "He's dead! I know it! He's dead, he's dead, he's dead!"

"He's *not* dead, Princess," Jerry Gundersen told his daughter firmly that evening as he sat on the edge of her bed. "There's not a reason in the world to assume Richard's dead." He spoke to her calmly, reassuringly, relieved that the hysterics in which he had found her when he picked her up at the Rotary Club meeting had subsided. She had quieted down as soon as she had seen her father, as if she did not wish to embarrass him with her emotions. Now she was nodding obediently as he spoke. "Let's go over it again, Sharon," he said patiently. "Richard's beeper went off twice, right?"

"Right."

"Now you know that a beeper isn't activated unless a chute opens and if his chute opened, it means Richard got out of the plane."

"But, Daddy," she looked at him quizzically, "couldn't

the beeper have been set off by accident, you know, just some wires goin' off by themselves, or"—she paused— "from the force of the plane bein' hit?" Her voice was barely audible.

Jerry looked at her suspiciously. Who the hell had she been talking to? "It could be, sure, honey. You know as well as I do about that woman in Texas whose husband went down. They never heard his beeper at all, and then after three years she got a letter from him in prison camp. A mechanical failure in the beeper, it turned out. Things like that happen sometimes, but hell, the odds are with you. If Richard's beeper went off, it means he more than likely got out."

She spoke quietly. "Then why didn't any of the wing men see him?"

"Hell!" Jerry exploded. "Do you know how hard it is to see anything in the midst of a gun battle in the air? You're lucky to get out of it alive yourself. With the enemy down there firin' up at you, you're not too careful about looking beneath you for open parachutes. Easiest thing in the world to miss a flier bailing out," he told her emphatically.

"Daddy?" She looked at him supplicatingly. Innocently, he thought, like a child. "What do *you* think? What do you *really* think happened to Richard?"

He took a deep breath. "Sharon, honey, the Pentagon has told forty thousand families in this country that their boy is dead. They've told 'em without flinching from the task. Now do you honestly think that if they had reason to believe Richard was dead, they would keep it from *you?*" He cupped her chin in his hand the way he used to do when she was a little girl.

"Okay, Daddy." She smiled at him.

"Feel better, Princess?"

For a second, she didn't answer him; then she gave him her habitual nod.

That night, she lay awake late in her four-poster bed, unable to sleep. Her outburst at the Rotary Club had terrified her, not only because she had voiced the hitherto forbidden thought that Richard was dead, but because, for the first time in her life, she had completely lost control of herself. What was happening to her? she wondered in panic, staring at the ceiling. The face of Ed Baldwin, telling her Richard was dead, floated before her eyes and then was pushed out of her mind's view by the face of her father. They wouldn't let her alone; they wouldn't let her believe one thing, or the other.

She had to get out, she suddenly thought to herself. She had to have a place of her own, for herself and Ricky. Her present life, she saw in a flash of clarity, was destroying her. But how would she do it? An apartment or a house? She didn't even know how much she could afford to spend. Her father mustn't know, she realized, or he would try to stop her. A car, she thought. She would need a car. That would be the first thing to do. With a car she could look for a place and then tell her parents when everything was arranged.

Excited by her plan, she finally fell into a restless sleep.

"What type model did you have in mind?" The salesman, balding, a slight pouch protruding over his belt, smiled at her.

"Oh, I don't know, just a car—somethin' not too big, and not too small." She glanced nervously around the showroom.

"Well, let's see." The salesman followed her eyes, trying to guess her desires. "Could you give me just a *little* bit more of a clue? Do you want a two-door, a four-door, a hardtop, a convertible, a station wagon?"

"Maybe you could just show me some cars?" She smiled at him to cover her uncertainty, and he obediently led her around the showroom, extolling the unique features of various floor models. "How about this one, Mrs.— Dornbeck, did you say your name was?" Sharon nodded. "I could give you this model at a very special price. It's not too big—and not too small." He laughed, pleased with himself. "You have children?" he asked.

"Yes, one little boy."

"Well, I'm sure your family will grow, and this car'll be plenty big enough for all the Dornbecks." He beamed at her, but she said nothing. "You can get it complete with power steering and brakes for the sticker price." He paused and looked at her. A beautiful girl, he thought, but peculiar. "Do you *like* this car?" he finally asked.

"Oh, yes," she nodded, as if her thoughts had been elsewhere.

The salesman was puzzled. Usually customers pursued him if they were really interested, bargained, argued, or walked away in disgust. This woman seemed devoid of any of those responses. "Well, shall we write it up, then?" He smiled encouragingly at her.

"Well, I don't know. . . ."

"Mrs. Dornbeck, you know this is a handsome model, white walls and leather seats—sort of sporty." He winked at her. "I bet your husband would like that look. Are you going to surprise him with the car?"

"Surprise him?" She looked surprised herself. "Oh, no, this is for me."

"Oh." The salesman searched for a new tack. "How about air conditioning? I could give you air conditioning on this car for very little extra."

"Air conditioning?" Her eyes looked vacantly at him.

"Yes." He paused. There was something very odd about this woman. "And you can also have automatic driver-controlled push-button windows for not much more. . . ."

She nodded at this as she had at almost everything he had said.

"Perhaps you would like a tape deck?" he inquired.

"A tape deck?"

"Yes, you know, to listen to cassette music. And cruise control is optional of course, but I would recommend it for the highways around here."

He saw her hesitate, as if she were struggling to figure out something. Then she turned to him, and he felt that she had finally made up her mind about the car because she seemed suddenly more alert. "You know, sir," she said to him, her voice more animated, "I'm afraid I really don't know too much about cars. I should have brought my husband in here with me in the first place. He's the one knows all about those things in our family."

"Well, fine, Mrs. Dornbeck. Why don't you bring him in? We're open every night until nine."

"I'll do that," she smiled at him. "He'll be home at suppertime, and we'll both be in this evenin'. 'By now."

Sharon felt genuinely relieved as she took the bus back home. She never should have tried to buy a car alone, and she knew there was some reason why she hadn't wanted her father to help her. Her husband was the one who should have gone with her. She could hardly wait to bring Richard back to the showroom that evening.

23

Letter from the Department of the Air Force

Dear Air Force Next of Kin,

We recently learned that ———————, a Brazilian journalist, visited North Vietnam and was given a number of letters from American prisoners of war which were to be mailed to their next of kin. It is our understanding that a letter from your husband was included.

All of the other Air Force next of kin involved have already contacted us to advise that they had received the letters and would forward them to us as they have done in the past. However, since we have not heard from you, we decided to write to you and offer our assistance in locating your husband's letter in the event it has not been received. If the letter has arrived in the mail, please forward it to us with any comments you may have about the contents. A self-addressed envelope is included for that purpose. Although we well realize that letters from prisoners are the private property of the next of kin, we consider it essential that they be scruti-

nized for any comments which conceivably
could have a hidden meaning. If such is the
case with your husband's letter, we possibly
would be able to lessen the anxieties of
another next of kin, which we believe is a
most important consideration.

For the continued protection and welfare of
American prisoners of war, we urge you not
to discuss the contents of this letter outside
of your immediate family. Be assured that
we will continue to expeditiously contact
you whenever we receive additional information pertaining to your husband.

The night before Julie Buell's First Communion, Mary
Kaye carried her daughter's stiffly starched white dress up
the stairs. Tiptoeing into the child's room, she hung the
dress on the doorknob; puff-sleeved and stiff, possessed
almost of a life of its own. Carefully she laid out Julie's
white socks, black patent-leather shoes, lace-trimmed panties and white eyelet slip on top of the dresser. As she
looked down at her daughter sleeping in the lower bunk
bed, Mary Kaye suddenly felt overwhelmingly tired. It was
not just the fact that she had done a spit-and-polish clean-
ing of the house and readied her troop's clothes for church
the next day. This was more a spiritual fatigue, which she
experienced as a seductive desire to let go, to lower her
defenses, her efforts to be strong, the way a runner far
out in front in a race feels when he sees the goal in sight
and knows that he can run easy now. I have done it, Mary
Kaye thought, looking at Julie sleeping so quietly. The
last First Communion, the last white dress, the last blue
suit. Four good Catholic kids. I have endured, she thought
to herself. I have done it alone.
　She went into her room and sat down in front of her
glass-topped dressing table. Resting her chin on her palms,
elbows on the table, she stared down at the pictures of
Brian trapped beneath the glass, trapped in time. Brian in

his flight suit, rugged and tanned, Brian and she posing for a formal wedding picture, she so thin and short-haired, Brian stiff-necked and awkward in the unaccustomed tuxedo. He looked lean-bodied and very young. She stared hard into the mirror in a way she did not often permit herself to do. Under her eyes, tiny cobwebs of lines were beginning to spin outward. Below her nose, two almost invisible creases crept downward toward her mouth. She thought back to a recent picture story in *Look* showing Margaret Holroyd waving good-by to her children as they left for school. The caption under it had read, "Margaret Holroyd, looking old beyond her thirty-one years . . ." and Mary Kaye had thought how cruel the wording was. She put her fingertips to her temples and pulled the skin of her face taut, erasing the lines, smoothing out the years. She looked long and hard at her face.

"Mom?" Pete's voice came from the doorway. Quickly she picked up a lipstick and started to apply it. "How long've you been standing there?" she asked him, looking at his reflection in the mirror, serious-eyed in his pajamas.

"Mom, you know Dad's five years older too."

She turned and grinned at him, touched at his surprising perception, and when she spoke her voice was that of a tough drill sergeant. "Pete, if we get through this thing alive, I'm gonna get you a DFC."

"I think we're doing okay, don't you, Mom?"

"I sure do."

He didn't move from the doorway. "You busy?"

"No, come on in." Mary Kaye watched him settle himself on the edge of her king-sized bed, one ankle hooked under the other knee in the casual acrobatics of childhood. "We were talking about some stuff in current events," Pete began in that special voice he reserved for talking to equals and his mother, "ecology and all that, and Neil, this guy in my class, brought in this article about how we've defoliated Vietnam and parts of the land will never be fertile again." He looked up at his mother. "Do you believe that?"

"I've read about it, too."

Pete began picking the toenail of his big toe. "I don't think Daddy knew about that when he went over, do you?"

She felt him waiting for her answer. "No, honey, I don't think he did. Daddy didn't know about a lot of things when he went over." They sat quietly for a moment. "Hey, Petey"—she had not called him that since he was a baby— "give me a kiss goodnight?" He shuffled off the bed and bending over his mother seated on the low dressing-table chair, brushed an embarrassed kiss on her cheek. "G'night, Mom."

"G'night, son."

The chords of the organ echoed strong and solemn through the church, and in the pews everyone sat up a little straighter and leaned forward to get a better view. Mary Kaye always loved this sense of expectancy at a First Communion. It was like the moment at a wedding just before the bride appeared and everyone waited to see her, imagining her emotions, sharing her expectations. The children rustled. On one side of the aisle, the girls stood up, fluffing up their crinolines, remembering to fold their hands. Across the aisle, the boys slid off their seats to a standing position, moving their heads like nervous turtles inside unaccustomed shirt collars.

Mary Kaye saw Jamie Holroyd, chestnut hair in a pompadour wave, hands clutching the black prayer book. In the pew across from Mary Kaye, Margaret Holroyd sat watching her eldest son, tears already beginning to course down her cheeks. This was Margaret's first First Communion, and Mary Kaye knew how she felt. Margaret had one arm around each of her other two children, and completing the family grouping, on either side of Amy and Billy Holroyd were Margaret's white-haired parents. The choir began singing, and the communicants started to file out, one boy and one girl together walking down the aisle, a young and very pure bridal couple.

Dear Mary Kaye,
This January we will be married thirteen years. Remember the time we took the kids to Disneyland?

Joe was so scared on the Matterhorn. Was that our
sixth anniversary or our seventh? I like to think back
to those times. . . .

Mary Kaye watched her daughter lead the girls' line, the
white veil covering her dark bangs and button nose, only
her curls visible from the back pews. Julie was approach-
ing the altar now, kneeling, opening her mouth to receive
the wafer.

I guess I wouldn't know the children any more. Does
Joe still like to walk up the slide backwards? Is Pete
still Dennis the Menace? Does Kathy still look like
you? I hope so. Julie's First Communion must be this
year. We have no more babies, you and I. . . .

No more babies. . . . Mary Kaye thought back to the
day Julie was born. A spring morning like this one, fresh
and crisp. They were living in a cramped apartment almost
forty minutes from Chester, and her labor pains had begun late at night. Brian was asleep next to her in the bed,
and she lay in the breezy darkness of the room, her belly
large in front of her, silently clenching and unclenching
her fists, determined to make no noise, determined not to
wake him. When the other babies had been born, she and
Brian were always separated. Though standard procedure
in military hospitals, she had always intensely resented
this separation: yet another intrusion of the military into
the intimacy of husband and wife. This time she vowed
that Brian would be with her. Through the long hours of
the early morning, she labored quietly, hearing the tick of
the alarm clock loud in her ears, softly panting with the
pains as her husband slept peacefully next to her.
When she knew the baby was coming very soon, she
awakened him and told him it was time to go to the base
hospital. "It's coming very fast," she told him in the car
as he sped along. "I guess with the fourth it's very fast."
When they were still ten minutes from Chester, she told
him to stop the car. "Brian darling, I'm afraid this baby
won't wait." She remembered how scared he'd been, and

how calm she was, even through the pain. He had pulled the car off the road into a tree-screened patch; and there, as the sun rose blood-red and new over them, in the front seat of their car, Brian had reached his hands into her and pulled out his daughter, his Julie. It was the only time she had ever seen him cry, and she thought as she lay back laughing through her tears, watching the baby wriggle in his arms, that that moment was as close to ecstasy as she would ever know.

She watched her daughter seat herself again in the pew, bow her head and pray.

For Thanksgiving this year we had a good meal,
turkey and real coffee. You know how I love coffee.
Send me warm clothes. It's so cold here this year. . . .

Mary Kaye looked over at the statue of the Blessed Virgin at the corner altar, decorated now with white flowers in honor of the month of May, the month of Mary. Surely, she thought, there are lessons to be learned. Surely this is not all in vain. Along with her daughter, Mary Kaye bowed her head and silently prayed.

"Don't forget to tell Daddy I led the girls' line," Julie called to her mother that evening after dinner.

"I won't." Mary Kaye was seated at the polished maple dining-room table, a piece of furniture reserved for formal occasions and which she somehow felt was an appropriate desk for her letters to Brian. The communion clothes were put away, and everyone had returned to the slacks, popsicles, and bickerings of normal life.

"Mom, can I watch *F Troop?*" Kathy called in from the living room.

"Negative."

"Why not, Mommy?"

"Because *F Troop* is on at 2100 and your bedtime is 2030. Pete?" Pete stuck his head around the corner. "Pete—"

"I know, did I do my homework, right?"

"Psychic, the boy is psychic!" She smiled at him. "No

more TV until you've finished." He gave her a disgusted look and headed upstairs. "And tell Joe to wash the ring around the tub," she called up to him. "Julie, Kathy, get rid of the wrapping paper and put away the communion presents. And, lady," she turned to Julie, "tomorrow we sit down together and write thank-you notes."

"Yuck!" Julie made a face.

Julie and Kathy were still gathering wrapping paper and Mary Kaye had almost finished her letter to Brian when the doorbell rang. She put the pen down. "I'll get it," she called to the children.

Colonel Lloyd and a military chaplain stood on the doorstep. Mary Kaye had a crazy feeling that this had all happened before, that there had been some peculiar throwback in time to the day in 1965 when the same two had stood before her to tell her Brian was missing. She looked at them, puzzled.

"Mrs. Buell . . ." Colonel Lloyd was speaking. "The Swedish government has just released a list received from Hanoi." She felt the blood beginning to pound in her head. Was Brian coming home? "It's my sad duty to tell you that your husband, Captain Brian Buell, has died in prison camp." Her knees buckled under her, and the chaplain caught her as she fell.

"Mommy?" Julie Buell was calling. "Mommy, who's at the door?"

24

**Letter from Department of Air Force to
Wife in New York**

I am writing to pass a special interest item
to you in the event you may be or plan to
be in the Pasadena, California, area on the
Fourth of July.

We have been advised by the Department of
Defense that a "Salute to American Servicemen" (a patriotic theme) will be held in the
Rose Bowl at Pasadena between 7:00 and
10:00 p.m., 4 July 1970. We understand
that the Lieutenant Governor will be the
main speaker, and that a number of other
notables have been invited. There will also be
an outstanding display of fireworks. As an
adjunct to the proceedings, the entire ceremony will be dedicated to those military
members who are missing in action or
prisoners in Southeast Asia.

The affair is being sponsored by a number
of civic groups. They have invited the family
members of those to whom the ceremony
will be dedicated to be their guests for this
event. . . .

As with past gatherings, we want to remind
you that government funds are not available
to next of kin for attendance at the Rose
Bowl, and that arrangements for and cost of
transportation and accommodations are the
responsibility of the traveler. . . .

Outside the Florida sun was hot and bright, but in Mary
Kaye's living room the shade had been pulled down to
muffle the light. She had drawn them herself that morning,
an instinctive gesture because the day's clarity and promise
had seemed almost an affront to her feelings. Around the
edges of the shades, sunlight still flickered into the room,
but now it was muted. Mary Kaye sat on the worn club
chair, feet up on the coffee table, hands hanging down
limply from the chair's arms. Her eyes were puffed and
red. She felt played out, exhausted. A dull pain persisted,
unconfined, unlocatable, not in her head or throat or
chest but in all of her, as if she had been hit so totally
that she no longer could tell exactly where it ached. The
suspense was ended, and it had all been for nothing. Not
until Colonel Lloyd had told her just a few hours ago—
less than one day ago—that Brian was dead, had she
realized how much she was counting on his return. She
picked up a telegram from Brian's cousin, glanced at its
message of sympathy and threw it onto the coffee table.
The price of hope was too high, she thought. Anger and
despair were cheaper.

The phone rang, and Pete quickly ran in to answer it.
"Hello? . . . Just a minute. Mom, it's Mrs. York." Mary
Kaye leaned back in her chair, staring at nothing, and
shook her head. "She doesn't want to talk now," Pete explained. "Can you call back tomorrow? . . . Aunt Joanne
came and got Julie and Kathy. . . . Okay, I'll tell her. 'By."
He turned to his mother. "She wanted to know if she
could take the girls overnight."

"Thanks, Petey." She smiled slightly at him.

When she had told the children that their father was
dead, the only one who cried was Julie. "But where *is*

Daddy now?" she had asked tearfully. "Is he still in Vietnam?"

"He's in heaven," Kathy had told her.

"I know his soul's in heaven," Julie had answered, "but won't they even send his body home from Vietnam? Can't we even bury him the way we buried Chippy?" Julie's pet canary was more real to her than her father, Mary Kaye thought. The other children had not cried; they had only been unusually quiet. Joe had said nothing at all to her since the news came. He had only stayed in his room. It was as if the children felt no sting at the death of their father, his absence having been so close to death for them. What is death to a child, she thought, except non-presence?

"Mom?" Pete was seated on the couch, elbows on his dungarees, chin in his hands. "Are we going to school tomorrow?"

"I don't think so. Why, do you want to?"

"No, but—it's— Never mind."

"Pete," she said, "I know what you're getting at. Daddy hasn't been here for five years, so what's so different about tomorrow. Is that it?"

"I don't care about school," Pete tried to explain, afraid he had upset his mother further.

"That I know too well, dear heart," she said, a flicker of the old acerbity in her voice.

"No, Mom . . ."

"Pete, it's okay. I understand. You'll stay home one more day."

The doorbell rang, and Pete got up to answer it. "I don't want to see anybody," Mary Kaye called to him.

"Sandy, hi!" she heard Pete's voice at the door.

"Is it Sandy?" Mary Kaye called, getting up from her chair. "Sandy, come in!" Wordlessly they embraced, and for a long moment Sandy held the larger woman in her arms as Mary Kaye's body shook. "What am I gonna do, San?" They sat down together on the couch. "Oh, God, what am I gonna do?" Mary Kaye pressed her palms to her eyes and brought herself under control again. "I've prepared myself for it so many times," she said to Sandy.

"For five years I've been telling the kids it could happen. But now . . ."

"What was it," Sandy asked softly, "malaria?"

"I don't know. They just said 'disease.'"

"Mom," Pete said awkwardly, "we'll manage. We'll be okay."

"Sure you will," Sandy smiled up at him.

"Pete, go see where Joe is. Tell him it's lunchtime," Mary Kaye ordered him. "Poor Pete," Mary Kaye turned to Sandy, "he's like a little old man—trying to take over Joe's job. Right before going to Vietnam, Brian said to Joe, very casually, 'You'll be the man of the house until I'm back.' The kid was only seven years old, for God's sake!" She shook her head. "Sandy, I want to tell you something."

"Mary Kaye, don't talk now. Wait till you feel better."

"No, I've got to tell this to someone." She took a deep breath, steadying herself to go on. "When Brian went to Vietnam for the second tour, he didn't have to go. He didn't have to go, Sandy. He *volunteered*. I was so angry, I screamed at him, I yelled at him—I even threw the coffeepot at him!" She gave Sandy a quick tearful smile. "I did! I told him if he went over again, I'd divorce him. That's the last thing I said to him. I didn't even drive him to the airport!"

"Oh, but he knew you didn't mean it. Mary Kaye, you wrote him for five years!"

"But I never knew if he got my letters. You know what *his* were like. I put something in every letter like 'I will always be your wife,' but how do I know he got them? Sandy, I never even drove him to the airport! And when I first heard he was in prison camp, I thought, serves him right for leaving me again! But I didn't mean it." She looked at Sandy imploringly, as if by convincing Sandy she could convince her dead husband. "I didn't mean it. I always loved him. Goddamn!" She shook her head. "For him to hang in there for five years and *then* die—it seems so unfair!" Sandy silently held Mary Kaye's hand.

"Mom." Mary Kaye looked up sharply. Joe was standing in the doorway, a cup of steaming liquid in his hand.

The hair from his cowlick was sticking up in back, and he seemed embarrassed. "Mom?" He held the cup toward her. "It's Campbell's Cream of Mushroom."

She realized that he had heard everything she had said to Sandy. With surprise, she saw that Joe, who she thought had not taken his father's death very hard, must have been crying earlier. "Thanks, Joey," she said.

"You like Cream of Mushroom," he explained.

"Put it here." She cleared a spot on the coffee table. Her eyes felt so tired. "I'll get to it in a little while." So it took this, she thought.

"Okay, Mom." He looked at her for a minute, as if he wanted to say something more. "You need a napkin?" he asked finally.

She shook her head. "That's okay, Joey. Everything's fine. Everything's just fine." She watched him walk out of the room, his hands jammed in his pockets, his head down, and she wanted to run after him and hug him. But her legs felt drained of strength, and it seemed more than she could do to move. There would be time for that, she thought. Gratefully she picked up the cup of soup.

Three days later a special funeral mass attended by family, friends, and military personnel was held for the soul of Brian Buell. This was meant not only as a religious ceremony, but also to provide an official ending, to give a needed air of finality, to his life. However, the mass itself seemed almost an extension of the state of limbo in which Brian had been living. The funeral, after all, had been occasioned by an announcement from the Swedish government. There was, moreover, no visible body at Brian's death just as there had been no visible body, as far as his family was concerned, for the last five years of his life.

Mary Kaye later made repeated attempts to find out the circumstances of her husband's death and what in fact had happened to his body. She wrote to the North Vietnamese delegation, to the Red Cross, and to other prisoners who had been released later. But she was never able to determine if Brian had been given last rites, or where he had been buried. Or even if he had been buried.

Joe, Pete, Kathy, and Julie Buell, however, were certain that their father was resting peacefully on a grassy hillside in a small village outside Hanoi. Their mother had even pointed out the spot to them on a map.

25

Fletcher Gibbs often remarked to his colleagues at the Pentagon that the craziest thing about this crazy war was that it had no predictable pattern—not to the fighting, not even to North Vietnam's occasional release of prisoners. In the course of 1968 and 1969, the North Vietnamese government voluntarily released nine men, six from the Air Force and three from the Navy. As far as Gibby or anyone else at the Pentagon could tell, there was no particular reason for the freeing of these nine: none was particularly high level—one, in fact, D. B. Hegdahl, was a seaman who had simply had the ill luck and bad balance to fall overboard into the North China Sea—and none was especially sympathetic to his captors. Pure caprice seemed to be at work, and it was this very caprice, this randomness about the fate of the prisoners which kept the families hoping and which kept the American government from being surprised at any moves the North Vietnamese might make.

For this reason, the following news release caused no particular astonishment—to Gibby, at least.

PARIS, *July 20 (UPI)—North Vietnam today announced the release of three American fliers held as prisoners of war: Captain Trumbull Porter of Sioux City, Iowa, Colonel Floyd McCabe of Peoria, Illinois, and Lieutenant Roy Lawton of Tampa, Florida. The men were released yesterday morning and will be flown*

188

to Saigon some time today. No reason for the release was given.

Ambassador Ellsworth Bunker, when asked to comment, replied that the release of the prisoners did not mark any significant advance in negotiations but said, "Naturally we are delighted to learn of this development."

TAMPA, *Florida, July 21—Mrs. Roy Lawton, wife of the Air Force lieutenant freed yesterday by the North Vietnamese after almost three years in captivity, said today that she was totally surprised at her husband's release. "Of course, I am overjoyed," Mrs. Lawton added.*

26

From a Press Conference with President Nixon

Question: Mr. President, the United States' position has been that North Vietnam has not genuinely offered the release of American prisoners, but rather only to discuss the release of American prisoners.

My question is: does your rejection of setting a deadline for the withdrawal of American troops include the possibility that North Vietnam might in the future offer the actual release of American prisoners rather than simply the discussion of that question?

The President: You very well have put the problem that we are always confronted with. You may recall very well that when President Johnson ordered the bombing halt it was the assumption that the North Vietnamese would negotiate seriously on ending the war. They didn't do it.

So a promise to discuss means nothing from the North Vietnamese. What we need is far more than that. We need action on their part and a commitment on their part with regard to the prisoners.

> Consequently, as far as any action on our
> part of ending American involvement com-
> pletely—and that means a total withdrawal is
> concerned—that will have to be delayed until
> we get not just the promise to discuss the
> release of our prisoners, but a commitment
> to release our prisoners because a discussion
> promise means nothing where the North
> Vietnamese are concerned.

Rain was pummeling Mary Kaye's red Pontiac in a fast staccato, slapping against the windshield and sides of the car in great wet sheets. Along the sides of the highway, palm trees bent over, pleading before the fury of the storm. From the car it was impossible to see beyond the palm trees, the rain obliterating even the usual sight of honky-tonk billboards. It was a blinding tropical storm, violent and intense, the way Brian used to describe the rains in Vietnam. The kind of weather he had hated to fly in, Mary Kaye recalled; the kind of weather she wished now she didn't have to drive in. Yet despite the storm, there had been no question that Mary Kaye would drive Sandy to the Tampa airport for the flight to Washington. It was understood, without any words being exchanged between them, that just as Sandy had helped Mary Kaye through Brian's death, Mary Kaye would be with Sandy through Roy's rather more protracted return to life.

On the front seat next to Mary Kaye, Sandy sat holding a navy patent bag, her trench coat damp from the rain, a daisy-covered folding plastic rain hat covering her hair. Margaret Holroyd and Jane York were in the back. They had asked to come, and Sandy had agreed. If Roy could make it, so could John Holroyd; so perhaps could Earl York, whom Jane still had not heard from in over four years.

"You think the plane'll take off in this weather?" Jane asked.

"If it doesn't, we'll hijack it and fly it ourselves. Right, Mary Kaye?" Margaret asked.

"Right." Silence settled over the car again, broken only by the steady noise of the rain and the thwack-thwack of the windshield wipers. Mary Kaye reached over and took Sandy's hand. "Your hands are like ice, San. Shall I put the heater on?"

"I'm okay."

Mary Kaye concentrated on the road again, not ungrateful for the long stretches of silence. Later, she planned to drive over to the Gundersens. Sharon, back from the private sanitarium in Orlando, could have visitors briefly now and had specifically asked to see Mary Kaye.

"I just can't believe it." Margaret gave Sandy's shoulders a slight squeeze. "After all these years, it's over for one of us."

"For two of us," Mary Kaye added.

"Oh, God, Mary Kaye, I *am* sorry." Margaret settled back uneasily and the silence returned.

Sandy looked down at her nails. Polish. For the first time in almost three years she was wearing polish. "Blush pink," the color she had used when she and Roy were married. Her hair, which she had been letting grow ever since she met Alan, was now swept up into a beehive, the way she used to wear it. In a recurring dream she had been having, Roy walked off the plane tanned and handsome, his honeymoon self, looked at her and walked right past her. "Where's Sandy? Where's my wife?" he asked everyone at the airport.

"Hey, Sandy," Jane asked, "what did you finally decide to wear?"

"My blue suit." Sandy unbuttoned her trench coat to show a white piqué-collared navy blue suit, trim and unobtrusively passé. "You think that's okay?"

"You look great!" Jane smiled at her. In the end the fantasies about wearing transparent blouses and skintight jump suits had been abandoned. She had no desire to appear sexy or modish, only familiar and reassuring.

"You'll just have to take it slow," Tony Vinza had warned. *"Most men are confused, disoriented when they come home. Don't spring too many changes on him. . . ."*

Just be yourself, the way you were when he left you. That's what he married, and that's what he's been dreaming of returning to. . . ."

A truck passed their car, sending up a blinding spray of water against the windshield, and Sandy blinked instinctively.

"Do you think we'll ever know why they released him?" Jane asked.

"Oh, let a few rot to death, release a few, that's the way they do things," Mary Kaye replied bitterly.

"Do you think you can just go back and pretend nothing has happened?"

"What can I do, Alan, I'm his wife."

"It's no good, Sandy, you're fooling yourself. The little girl Roy married no longer exists. He'll know it the first time he talks with you, he'll sure as hell know it the first time he sleeps with you. . . ."

Mary Kaye signaled for a right-hand turn. "Here we go, ladies—a half-mile to the airport. Neither rain nor snow can keep us. . . ." She leaned forward in her seat and squinted to see the signs in the rain.

"Sandy dear," her mother had written, "Dad and I want you to have this check for $500 to use for a second honeymoon. We can't make up for lost time, but we're looking forward to getting to know our son-in-law. . . ."

"I wonder how he'll look," Jane York said softly. Margaret glared at her. There had been a tacit understanding not to mention anything as real as that. "Remember when Frishman was released," Jane continued, unaware, "he lost forty-five pounds."

"They gain it back fast once they're home," Mary Kaye announced in a firm voice which silenced Jane.

Sexual problems are not uncommon in returning prisoners, Major Rosen had said. Problems of impotency have been well noted in the literature, and of course we do not know what exposure the prisoner may have had to homosexual contact . . .

"I wonder if Gibby will be at Andrews," Margaret was saying.

"Are you kidding? Would Gibby miss it?" Mary Kaye

piped up. "Holy God, he'll probably have the United States Marine Band, a color guard, and a drill team. Gibby miss a chance like that?"

Through the rain, Sandy saw the sign DEPARTING PASSENGERS and felt her stomach tighten. She tried to imagine Roy in an airplane now, somewhere over the middle of America, speeding toward his meeting with her in Washington. She could picture the airplane, even imagine it on a map suspended somewhere above Illinois. But she could not get a picture of Roy inside it. She seemed unable to put a face on top of a uniform.

"Alan, he needs me."

"I need you too. Or don't I count? Don't you love me?"

"Yes, Alan, yes. But what does that have to do with it?"

They pulled up by the curb now, and Mary Kaye cut the motor. "Stay inside, San," she directed. "It doesn't matter if I get wet." Mary Kaye, who never believed in rain hats or umbrellas, got out her side, opened the trunk of the car, oblivious to the downpour, and hauled out Sandy's suitcase. Margaret and Jane were out of the car already, holding umbrellas over their own heads and shielding the door for Sandy until she could raise her own umbrella. In one brief dash they reached the canopy and stood there for a moment breathlessly. "Whew! We made it!" Mary Kaye exclaimed, putting down Sandy's luggage and wiping the water from her cheeks.

The rain was beginning to slacken now, and other cars were arriving, disgorging passengers, hurrying along on their way. Margaret nudged Jane, who quickly took a florist's box from under her arm. "Sandy, here, we almost forgot." The other three women smiled as Sandy pulled aside the green paper and removed a spray of pale yellow-white orchids and the card, "In peace as in war, we're with you. The Three Musketeers." Tears filled Sandy's eyes as she looked up at them smiling at her.

"Why don't you wait until you're almost over Washington before you put it on," Margaret suggested. "It'll stay fresher."

Inside the terminal, the impersonal mechanics of flight went into operation. Sandy's luggage was checked, her ticket torn off by a perpetually cheerful young clerk. "Eastern announces the departure of Flight 55 for Washington, boarding now at Gate 3. . . ." Routine. Strictly a routine flight, which in no way involved her volition. She had only to surrender herself, to permit herself to be borne, involuntarily, to Dulles Airport, where a military car would take her to Andrews Air Force Base. It was all arranged; she had only to relax and play her part. Margaret and Jane gave her a quick hug. "Last call for Eastern's Flight 55. . . ."

"You okay?" Mary Kaye pulled Sandy aside and asked her softly.

"Oh, Mary Kaye, I'm so scared." The words came out in a rush.

Mary Kaye put her hands on Sandy's shoulders, as if by doing so she could give Sandy strength. "You'll be okay." Sandy nodded and took a deep breath. "I suppose in a way I had it easier," Mary Kaye said. Sandy hugged her quickly, then turned and headed toward the gate.

For General Fletcher Gibbs, there was no denying this was a big day. A big day. Three of his boys were coming home, one to Norton, one to McGuire, and one right here to Andrews, and if Gibby's efforts had absolutely nothing to do with the men's release, that did not in any way dampen his enthusiasm or his sense of accomplishment. "Hell, you can't tell me those guys don't respond to pressure," he had told Captain Burroughs in the Pentagon. "It's the only language they understand. Ya gotta hit 'em, hit 'em and hit 'em again," he pounded on his desk, "on the ground, in the air, through the mails—you can't tell me all those letters to Hanoi didn't have some effect—and sooner or later they give." He felt pleased with himself, as if all his speeches to civic groups, his pep talks to the wives, the endless strategy sessions in the Pentagon had somehow produced this momentous result; and if someone had told Gibby that between his frenetic efforts and the release of three men there was no cause and effect, only a bizarre fluke of fate, or perhaps some new p.r. gambit in the mind of a North Vietnamese general, Fletcher

Gibbs would have been outraged. War was based on strategy, and therefore the play was important. If one didn't believe that, then there was no longer any opportunity for heroism.

In a way, Gibby hoped Lieutenant Lawton wouldn't look too good. Not that he wished the poor guy ill, but it would show a complacent America what the Communists did to their prisoners.

Gibby glanced at his watch. The Air Force plane should be landing any minute now. It was a clear, bright day, and the wind broke the usual heat of Washington in early September. Gibby watched the American flag atop the terminal waving crisply in the breeze. On the field, scattered among the television crews and newspaper reporters, was a dazzling collection of brass and politicos. General Fitzsimmons, the Secretary of the Air Force, the Under Secretary of Defense . . . Gibby smiled to himself, thinking how good it would all look to that poor bastard Lawton. A hero's welcome, that was what he was being given, and hell, why not? Anyone who could endure three years in a North Vietnamese prison camp *was* a hero—not the kind of storm-'em-in-the-bunkers hero Gibby had grown up admiring in World War II but a hero nevertheless, a victim who had endured, and sometimes, Gibby thought, endurance itself can be heroic. Besides, the Pentagon needed heroes just now and it was clear that the public would be highly sympathetic to any returning prisoner.

"How ya doin'?" Gibby moved over to stand next to Sandy Lawton in front of the rope cordon separating the landing area from the crowd of press and military.

"Pretty good." Cute, he thought. A real cute girl. He smiled down at her, happy that in some small way he had helped bring about her husband's return.

Captain Burroughs came over to them. "They'll be landing in three minutes, General."

"Thanks, Willy." He turned to Sandy. "Three minutes to touchdown. And remember," he cautioned her, "no questions about the camp, the war, and the other prisoners until he's been debriefed. Clear?"

Sandy nodded. Her heart was beginning to pound now.

She scanned the sky. In the distance a tiny speck could be seen.

"Can we get an interview, Mrs. Lawton?" A reporter stuck a microphone in her face. She shook her head. "Mrs. Lawton is not giving any interviews," Gibby said firmly. The reporter hovered nearby, hoping she would change her mind. The plane was getting closer now. She heard shouted instructions, cameras beginning to roll. Crewmen came out onto the landing field, ready to guide the plane down.

"Keep camera two on the wife, Marv, stick with her all the way, right up until they meet. We'll get one and three to cover the plane." Remember to smile, she told herself, remember to smile.

She watched the plane grow bigger, more real, and wished her hands didn't feel so cold. It was dropping now, an ungainly steel bird getting ready to plant itself on the ground. The jet scream was deafening, but not as loud as the pounding of her own heart.

Crewmen rushed forward with a landing staircase and clicked it into place. The curved steel door swung open. Two military aides stepped out of the plane, bracketing the door, and reached their hands back toward the man still inside.

Slowly a lean, gaunt shadow of a man stepped out, supported by the aides on either side. He blinked a few times in the bright sunlight, and his face, with its sunken cheekbones and vacant eyes, had a confused expression, as if he didn't quite know what to make of the flags and the cameras and the people. Though he wore the Air Force uniform, it looked big on him, and his head seemed dwarfed by the military hat. His eyes were looking around now, but he seemed bewildered, as if he were having trouble decoding what he was seeing.

Sandy stood still, unable to move. The man on the landing platform turned slightly and his hollow eyes looked in her direction, though they didn't seem to focus. As the television cameras rolled on, the skeletal face blinked again, as if it had recognized someone it once knew. Gibby was jostling her arm, "Go on, Sandy." Involuntarily, her feet carried her toward the stranger across the field.

Television coverage of the POW's return pulled an audience almost as large as that for the second moon shot. Whether you were watching the scene in black and white or in living color, young Lieutenant Lawton's emotion was visible. In many homes in America, people wept at sharing his and Sandy's joy.

"After greeting his wife," the CBS announcer explained, "Lieutenant Lawton will spend the next two weeks in Andrews Hospital, where he will be given medical attention and debriefed. After this final separation, he and his young wife will be reunited."

In the living room of the Buell house in Silver Grove, Mary Kaye sat with Julie on her lap and the other three children around her, watching the scene at Andrews. "Is Sandy happy, Mommy?" Julie asked, tugging at her mother's blouse.

"Get your feet off the table, Pete," Mary Kaye said, and Julie noticed her mother's voice sounded hoarse.

In a small rooming house near Walton State, Alan Webber sat, also watching the television set, unable—though he tried—to take his eyes away, as Roy Lawton stepped off the stairs onto the landing field, and a girl with a blond beehive moved toward him, walking at first, then running, her arms outstretched into the space between them.

The television announcer's voice rose to a smooth windup. "With all the sad stories that have come out of Indochina these last months, it is nice to report one which has a happy ending."